Northern Eye
Spectacles
Island
The
Bridge
Stonehenge
The Ark
Southern Eye
Sandy
Beach
N
THE BIG
8
W
E
Atlantic

Maida's Little Camp

Maida's Little Camp

BY

INEZ HAYNES IRWIN

Author of
MAIDA'S LITTLE SHOP, MAIDA'S
LITTLE HOUSE, ETC.

GROSSET & DUNLAP
Publishers : : New York

MADE IN THE UNITED STATES OF AMERICA

To the Little Eleanor
Who Used to Play with
the Little Phyllis on
House Rock Beside the
Fairy Pond

CONTENTS

Maida's Little Camp

MAIDA'S LITTLE CAMP

CHAPTER I

THE LITTLE HOUSE HUMS

THE Little House brimmed with activity that sunshiny Monday morning early in August.

It was not that the day flamed with a sunshine like gold melted to air and shot with electricity that caused this excitement. Nor was it even that the whole household had arisen at the early hour of six o'clock. Nor was it yet that the parents, or relatives, both of the Big Eight and the Little Seven, had passed the week-end in the Little House. No, something much more thrilling and important than any of these accounted for that fever.

In brief, the Big Eight—the eight older children, who lived in the Little House—were leaving that day for a month's stay in a camp in the Adirondacks.

And so, excitement burned in everybody.

The Big Eight were milling nervously about; opening suitcases and taking things out, closing and locking them; then opening them again to put the same things back or to insert other objects, closing and locking them again. Every few minutes, one would say, "Oh, I wish we could start!" But almost immediately someone else would add, "But oh, how I hate to leave the Little House! It doesn't seem possible that we could have such good times anywhere else."

The grown-ups who took care not only of the Big Eight but of the Little Seven—they also lived in the Little House—were flying about too. But there was an object for their activity. Every movement meant something and showed a result. Unlike the Big Eight, they did not do the same thing again and again.

The Little Seven, who were to be left behind from this camping expedition, had got entirely out of hand in the excitement of farewell. They were running madly about the house, up and down the stairs, back and forth across the rooms, in and out through the doors. For the time being there was nobody to stop them.

The four colored folk, who helped in the work at the Little House, were almost as excited as the children. Zeke, the only man in the quartette, looking, despite his plumpness, very trim in his khaki chauffeur's uniform—importance spurting from every angle of his figure—was waiting for the order to load up with luggage one of the two beach wagons which stood in front of the house. Florabelle, his wife, was dressed in what the Big Eight recognized as her going to church clothes, a thin silk of black with big, white polka dots and a little round hat trimmed with white flowers. Overflowing through all her roly-poly brown body with a sense of happiness and importance, she had taken her place beside her husband and was awaiting orders. The two maids, Della and Poppy—slender, young girls, very black-eyed and very brown-fleshed in their trim, white summer uniforms—were hugging first one of the girls of the Big Eight and then the other. Obviously, they were torn between their sense of importance at being for a month the senior members of the domestic corps and a desire to go off with the party.

Bunny White and Robin Hood, who were in command of the expedition, sat under the big elm on the lawn talking.

Bunny was a young woman, so little and slender that she could easily have taken the part of a child in a theatrical performance. Everything about her seemed to accentuate that childlike quality; especially the gay brown eyes which, from under the curling eyelashes, shot such innocent, friendly glances; the little head covered with short brown curls and the dimples which, with every smile, played in and out of her pink cheeks.

The Big Eight would have been amazed to learn that Bunny was all of twenty-six years old. They would have innocently said sixteen.

Robin Hood—his real name was Robert

Hood—was a young man of about thirty. He was a great contrast to Bunny in that he was very tall. Also he was muscularly swift and strong. His eyes were so deep a blue as to be almost black and his hair was darker than Bunny's. His face, too, was much more quiet in expression than hers, although it could break into a sudden smile like a swift, brief flash of sun on water. He was handsome and he looked able.

In their separate ways Bunny and Robin Hood were, the Big Eight thought, remarkable people.

Bunny had written a series of stories called the *Little Gypsy* books. She had stayed at the Little House for long periods at a time. She had taught the children English literature and composition.

Robin Hood had accompanied two expeditions through primitive country; one to South America, the other to Africa. He had taught the children arithmetic, geography and history with side excursions into botany, astronomy, geology and archaeology. Both Bunny and Robin Hood were accomplished storytellers. The Big Eight—and the Little Seven for that matter—admired them equally.

Mrs. Dore, who was in charge of the Little House, had put on a hat of dark blue straw which matched her suit of dark blue silk, but not yet the jacket to her suit. She was giving all kinds of last directions to her mother, who was not going off on the month's camping trip. Every other minute she stooped to drop a kiss on the silver ripples of Granny Flynn's softly parted hair. "Remember, Mother," she kept saying in her firm, pleasant voice, "if you are troubled about anything, just call up the Big House."

Mr. Westabrook lived in the Big House. It was several miles north of the Little House—a great mansion of white marble, set in the midst of velvet lawns, ample gardens; spraying misty fountains; cool, lily-spotted pools. Peacocks strolled and strutted over the lawns. Deer roamed the generous, enclosed park. Wide-spreading forest surrounded all. The Big Eight thought it very beautiful, but not to compare with the Little House.

"If Mr. Westabrook is not there," Mrs. Dore went on, "his secretary will do anything you want."

Mrs. Dore interrupted herself to pick up Delia and to kiss her hungrily on her round, freckled, purple-pink cheeks and under her little, peaked pearly chin. "Oh, my lamb," she reproached herself, "how can I leave you?" She put Delia back in her mother's arms.

"And remember, Mother," she went on, addressing herself again to the tiny, silver-haired woman with her sparkling eyes of an Irish blue, her amusing, fairy godmother, down-curving nose and her up-turned, fairy godmother chin which almost met, "remember I'll call you up often. Remember, too, if you want to hear my voice, just go to the telephone and call me up. You'll find the number written in big black figures on a card hanging there."

Again she snatched Delia from her mother's lap, hugged and kissed her, placed her again in that warm, grandmotherly receptacle.

"And if you don't feel like getting the number, ask Della or Poppy to do it. You don't feel alarmed at my going away do you, Mother?"

"And why should I be afraid of your going away?" Granny Flynn demanded. "Sure and now I'll run the house the way I've always wanted. Anyway how could I ever be lonely with a house full of such pleasant, friendly people."

The Little House would be full of what Granny Flynn called "pleasant, friendly people," for Mr. Westabrook had invited the parents of the Little Seven to stay there while the Big Eight were away. Every morning one of the big comfortable Westabrook motors was to take the men to their work in Boston and at night bring them back. Mr. Westabrook had planned with the men to manage things so that they could spend their two weeks of vacation there.

CHAPTER II

MR. WESTABROOK SAYS GOOD-BYE

IN THE meantime, Mr. Westabrook was very busy talking with the parents who were scattered all over the Little House.

There were plenty of rooms for them to occupy. The Little House, built in 1645, was what all New Englanders call a Cape Cod cottage. That meant, among other things, that from the outside it might look very small, but inside it might spread out to a surprising amplitude.

Although Cape Cod cottages are much alike inside, they may be built on a small plan or a large one. The Little House, with which Mr. Westabrook's ancestors had replaced their first, temporary log cabin home, was small. You entered by a dignified and beautiful doorway which was an extension, on the front, of the actual house, like a little vestibule. Over this vestibule foamed and feathered a rosebush. Now, it was long past its bloom, but it was beginning to develop the rose-hips which later would touch it with tiny peaks of scarlet. Inside was a tiny hall and in front of you, as you entered it, a flight of stairs almost as steep as a ladder. On either side of the tiny hall was a square room, each exactly the same size. One of these rooms the Big Eight called the Map Room because here the walls were hung with maps and because a big globe stood on the center table. The other room the Big Eight called the Book Room because its walls were completely lined with books. Back of these stretched a living room as big as the Map Room, the Book Room and the hall put together. Back of the living room lay a room equally big—the dining room. Above in the main house were the bedrooms of the four girls of the Big Eight. But although the original Little House had been small, the present structure was almost spacious. Roomy ells, the Annex and the New Wing—both later additions —stretched to the right and left of the Little House. In one was—all very roomy—kitchen, storeroom and gymnasium; in the other the boys' rooms. Above were Granny Flynn's and Mrs. Dore's sleeping rooms, the sleeping rooms of the household crew and the nursery.

Mr. Westabrook entered first of all the Map Room. Here Arthur Duncan and his father were talking together.

Arthur Duncan, a boy in his middle teens, was the oldest, tallest and strongest of the Big Eight and the natural leader of them all. Father and son bore a strong resemblance to each other and anybody skilled in recognizing nationalities would note at once the strong Scottish infusion in their blood. Mr. Duncan was, himself, an American by birth, although both his parents had been Scots. He was a machinist by trade, a tall, strongly built, black-haired, black-eyed man, taciturn, and—Mr. Westabrook knew through Arthur—a great reader. Naturally, Mr. Westabrook had never told any of the Big Eight, not even his daughter, Maida, that of all the parents who visited the Little House he liked Mr. Duncan best.

Mr. Westabrook was a tall, big man with a powerful figure and a powerful head. Indeed, so powerful was that head, so thick the shag of hair that covered it, so striking the angle at which it was set on his shoulders that he had always been called "Buffalo" Westabrook. As at his entrance Mr. Duncan and Arthur arose, the little room seemed, for a moment, full of noticeable-looking, strongly built, dark males.

"Sit down," Mr. Westabrook bade the other two, "I want to have a little talk with you both. I hope, Mr. Duncan, you are satisfied with the progress Arthur is making."

"The lad's doing fine," Mr. Duncan declared. "Not that perhaps he couldn't do better if he studied longer and harder."

Mr. Westabrook smiled and Arthur shuffled a little sheepishly in his chair.

"I expect that's something that could be said about every child who has ever lived," Mr. Westabrook commented pleasantly. "But we have no complaints to make of Arthur. He studies hard. What we like best about Arthur is that he seems to enjoy studying."

"How anybody couldn't enjoy studying at the Little House—" Arthur said. Obviously unable to imagine such a being, he stopped abruptly.

"I wonder, Mr. Duncan," Mr. Westabrook went on, "if you have been thinking of what you'd like to make of your boy or if you have any plans for his education—his training, or whatever."

For an instant Mr. Duncan's dark, silent face showed a gleam of interested perplexity. "To tell you the truth, Mr. Westabrook," he said hesitantly, "I don't feel at all certain myself. I don't want the thing to happen to him that happened to me. I always wanted to do out-of-doors work, but somehow, before I knew what I was doing, I had become a machinist."

"What would you have liked to do, Mr. Duncan?" Mr. Westabrook asked.

"Gardening," Mr. Duncan answered promptly. "Gardening is in the blood."

Mr. Westabrook did not speak for a moment. Evidently he was thinking hard.

Mr. Duncan continued, "I'd like the boy to go to college. I've got a little fund saved up for it, but I don't know what he ought to train himself for."

"I think," Mr. Westabrook declared, "that you won't have to bother about that. I think you'll find that Arthur will help you settle that question. Under Mr. Hood's training, he is developing into—well something that will be connected with the out-of-doors. Don't you feel that way yourself, Arthur?"

"Oh, yes, sir!" Arthur agreed. "Archaeology." His voice deepened on that word with a kind of awed emphasis.

"I'll leave you now," Mr. Westabrook said, rising. "I want to have a little talk with all the parents. Remember, Mr. Duncan, that I'll do anything in my power to help Arthur into the work he wants."

The two men shook hands.

Mr. Westabrook crossed the tiny hall to the library. Here sat Mr. and Mrs. Lathrop with two more of the Big Eight; their children, Laura and Harold. Mr. and Mrs. Lathrop were well-to-do. When Mr. Westabrook first met them, he had liked them the least of any of the parents of the Big Eight. It seemed to him that Mr. Lathrop, who was much older than his wife, had no interest outside of making money and that Mrs. Lathrop had no interest outside of the social advancement of her children. And at first it had looked to him as if the children were just the pair that one could expect from such parents. But life at the Little House had developed Laura and Harold amazingly. And curiously enough, their growth had quickened their parents' development.

Laura and Harold had grown from pert, nondescript types into a very attractive pair. Not handsome, Harold, and not beautiful, Laura. Yet the one might, as a young man, become extremely handsome and the other, as a young woman, really beautiful. Both were blue-eyed and brown-haired. Both had erect, graceful figures. Harold had at first tended towards stockiness, but he loved every out-of-doors sport. Swimming, tennis and golf—and incessant exercise in the gymnasium—had done much for him. Laura had at first seemed to Mr. Westabrook a little too slender; her figure looked breakable. Now, though she was still a sylph, muscle had conquered that fragility; roses bloomed constantly in her cheeks. From her earliest childhood Laura had taken lessons in skating and fancy dancing. She was far and away the most graceful of the girls of the Big Eight.

As Mr. Westabrook entered, Mr. and Mrs. Lathrop arose. Mrs. Lathrop was not a handsome woman. She was thin, grey-haired, a little colorless—but you looked at her. Perhaps that was because she had an air of command. And her clothes—a very simple grey silk suit and a broad, grey hat with a single, white orchid—showed an elegance that no other Big Eight mother displayed.

Mr. Lathrop, grey-haired too, had a pleasing, portly middle-aged comeliness. But somehow he never seemed important when Mrs Lathrop was present.

Mrs. Lathrop advanced, holding out her hand. "Mr. Westabrook," she began— Suddenly her eyes filled with tears and her voice began to shake. "I have not had an opportunity to tell you," she faltered, "how grateful Mr. Lathrop and I are for what you have done for our children. You have made different people of them. I realize, as I look back upon it, that my own system tended to spoil them a little. You see I was not young when they were born and I was so proud of them—" She quavered and stopped.

It pleased Mr. Westabrook greatly that Harold and Laura both stepped forward, Laura to put her arm about her mother on one side, Harold to throw his arm across her shoulders on the other.

"There never was a better mother in the world!" Laura remonstrated indignantly. "Please don't believe her, Mr. Westabrook."

"She doesn't know what she's saying," Harold reinforced his sister.

"Of course I'm not going to believe your mother, Laura," Mr. Westabrook answered.

"If there's one thing I know when I see it, it's a good mother."

Mr. Lathrop also spoke, "Nonsense, Ellen," he said testily. "You devoted yourself to them to the exclusion of everything else."

"That's it!" Mrs. Lathrop insisted. "That's just what I did."

"The proof of the pudding is in the eating," Mr. Westabrook insisted smilingly. "You've turned out a fine pair. I thought I'd just step in here to ask you what you thought about their future training. I know you must have plans for them and I'd like to help you with those plans. That is if you need any help. I'm not talking about money. I know you can take care of that end of it. But it's only that I love them both and I'd like to feel that I'd had a little to do with their development."

"Oh, Mr. Westabrook," Mrs. Lathrop protested, "we don't feel that we can say much there. We look to you to advise us. Everything you've done for them has been perfect. Whatever suggestion you make for the future, we'll follow."

Mr. Westabrook beamed. "Very well, then," he concluded, "let's all be thinking it over—even you, Laura and Harold. It isn't anything that we must bother about for a year or two, but we should all keep it in mind."

CHAPTER III

MR. WESTABROOK SAYS MORE GOOD-BYES

IN THE living room sat Mr. and Mrs. Brine. The Big Eight thought this the most beautiful room in the house, with its massive beams, its huge old-fashioned fireplace, the old, white-painted cupboards all about it with their black-painted butterfly and Holy Lord hinges, its huge windows where the sun poured through gayly flowered chintzes, its desk and tables always holding bowls of flowers, its comfortable chairs.

Rosie Brine was the most picturesque of the Big Eight. She was all vivid colors, all satiny sheens, all sparkling lights. Her great eyes and her curling hair were jet black; her cheeks and lips vied in crimson with each other. Her flesh, her brows, her lashes showed a satiny gloss. Her eyes and her teeth shot sparkles. She was a tall girl for her age, very active and strong. Indeed, in all athletic sports, the boys always accepted her as an equal.

As Mr. and Mrs. Brine arose to greet him, Mr. Westabrook thought, as he had often thought before, that at Rosie's age Mrs. Brine must have looked exactly like Rosie. He noted with great satisfaction that Mrs. Brine was still an extremely handsome woman because he hoped that Rosie would always keep her looks. And it entertained him, knowing Rosie's passion for red, that there were touches of scarlet in Mrs. Brine's costume; a shining, red leather belt and bag, a red rose on her black straw hat, little tinkling red earrings. Mr. Brine, as might be expected, was a rather drab person with hair of no particular shade of brown and eyes of no particular shade of blue. But he had a look of efficiency. It was obvious that Mrs. Brine was the personality of the family but it was also obvious that Mr. Brine was its steering gear.

"Mr. Westabrook," Mrs. Brine burst out the instant he appeared, "what you have done for our daughter! Why, she's growing like a weed! How well she looks! And—" She caught herself up.

"And how beautiful," Mr. Westabrook added for her. "I'm glad you think so, for we regard Rosie as a kind of Exhibit A."

"And she's so happy!" Mrs. Brine went on.

"And why shouldn't she be!" Mr. Brine put in. "She says she feels as if she was living in a fairy tale all the time."

"Rosie's certainly satisfying to have about," Mr. Westabrook assured Rosie's parents. "She's a kind of thermometer. She's so candid and frank. She never conceals her emotions, so that I can always tell how things are going at the Little House by the way Rosie looks."

"She writes us very happy letters," Mr. Brine added.

"I just thought I'd have a moment's talk with you," Mr. Westabrook went on, "to ask you if you'd been thinking what you'd like Rosie to be or do when she's grown up."

"Oh, I'm going to leave that all to you, Mr. Westabrook," Mrs. Brine said impulsively. "I mean . . . I don't mean anything about money . . . Mr. Brine and I can take care of our daughter, but we want you to tell us what to do with her. You'd be wiser about that than we would."

"I'm sure that's not true," Mr. Westabrook declared vigorously, "but I'm glad to know that you think so. I can assure you that I'm giving it a great deal of thought and some day we three and Rosie—" Here he smiled down into Rosie's thoughtful face which immediately sparkled in response. "—must gather together and talk that all out."

Outside in the garden at the back—a gay carpet of August flowers enclosed in cedars—sat Silva and Tyma Burle with their Aunt Save and their Great-aunt Vashti.

All four were gypsies. From time immemorial, a group of gypsies had camped of summers in one corner of Mr. Westabrook's estate. He had known and loved them all his life. And Maida, his daughter, could remember no time when she did not know and love them too. Silva and Tyma were the children of a ne'er-do-well, gypsy father. Always a drunkard, Mr. Burle had become a widower at the birth of his last child, little Nesta. Soon afterwards, he had married a woman whom his two older children could not possibly respect. They ran away to their Aunt Save, who was in summer camp on the Westabrook estate, bringing their baby sister, Nesta, with them. At first, the situation had presented difficulties. But Mr. Westabrook sent for Mr. Burle and prevailed upon him to let all three children come to live in the Little House. This was not difficult as the stepmother was delighted to get rid of them.

Aunt Vashti was a remarkable-looking creature. The gypsies said that she was a hundred years old. Mr. Westabrook did not believe this, although he thought she might be ninety. She was little and shrunken and wrinkled, but full of an amazing vivacity and energy. Her sunken eyes still shot sparks of animation and her personality seemed as salty and gay as when she was young. She did not join in the conversation which followed but she emitted clucks of sympathy, nodded and smiled her understanding. Great-aunt Vashti wore a dress of white wool which came up in a rolling collar close to her chin and in tight-fitting sleeves to her finger tips. She wore on her curling, white hair a tam of cream-colored worsted. On her neck gleamed her great treasure—Mr. Westabrook had seen it all his life—a heavy gold chain from which hung engraved five-and ten-dollar gold pieces—one twenty-dollar piece, forming the central pendant.

Aunt Save, a pleasing, tanned, grey-haired woman, plump as a balloon, gave out somehow an air of sagacity and efficiency. When she moved, it was surprising, considering her bulk, how light, swift and vigorous were her motions. This day she was dressed in her best—a purple satin. She wore a hat made entirely of silver leaves. And she wore a great deal of silver jewelry; earrings, chain, bracelets, rings. The Big Eight thought she was a most majestic figure—as, indeed, she was. She was holding Nesta in her arms.

On the grass in front of the two women sat Silva and Tyma.

If it was true that Maida Westabrook was, strictly speaking, the most beautiful of the girls of the Big Eight, that Rosie was the most picturesque, that Laura was the most graceful, it was certainly true that Silva was the most interesting. Brown of smooth, straight hair and deep, narrow eyes; creamy of velvety flesh; pink of softly curved lips—she was like a tea rose. Her look was always lost in dreams. It gave to her beauty a quality of mystery.

Tyma looked as alert as Silva dreamy and still. His swift, intelligent blue eyes accented this quality—the more that they contrasted so vividly with his curling crisp hair which was jet black and with his skin which, winter and summer alike, was deeply tanned.

As Mr. Westabrook advanced across the grass, Silva and Tyma immediately arose. Baby Nesta jounced with joy. "Missa-Book! Missa-Book!" she called. "Missa-Book" was as near as she could say, "Mr. Westabrook." She held out her arms to him. This, Mr. Westabrook knew, was not so great a compliment as it seemed; for Nesta, who was the friendliest of babies, held out her arms to everybody. Mr. Westabrook smiled warmly, however, and took the little creature from Aunt Save's lap into his strong, accustomed grasp. Nesta adapting herself cozily to the change in situation, leaned her head against Mr. Westabrook's shoulder and presently put her thumb in her mouth.

"Bad little Nesta!" Silva exclaimed fondly, removing the thumb.

"Well, Aunt Save," Mr. Westabrook greeted his guest cheerily, "you look as well and as handsome as ever. How are you?"

"Fair to middling, Mr. Westabrook," Aunt Save agreed, "I'm getting older though—older every day."

"You don't believe that, Aunt Save," Mr. Westabrook accused her, "and it's no use your trying to tell it to me because I don't believe it either."

"Still and all, Mr. Westabrook," Aunt Save insisted smiling broadly, "I used to hold you in my arms just the way you're holding baby Nesta."

"Nonsense, Aunt Save," Mr. Westabrook accused her, "you're bragging. You know you were only a baby yourself."

Aunt Save smiled again, even more happily, "How are these two children of ours behaving?" she changed the subject.

"They always behave well," Mr. Westabrook answered, throwing an arm about Silva's shoulders and drawing her toward him. "Better children there couldn't be anywhere. Glad to have this little chance to talk with you, Aunt Save. What do you want to make of them?"

"God bless my soul, Mr. Westabrook," Aunt Save answered with her pleasant familiarity. "I don't know what to do with them. Of course, I realize they're spoiled for gypsies. But I guess either you or they must settle that matter. Anything you want or they want is all right with me. You three just make up your minds and tell old Aunt Save and she'll give you her blessing."

"I knew you'd be the trump you've always been, Aunt Save," Mr. Westabrook applauded her heartily. "There's no hurry but we'll all be thinking about it and some day we'll come and have a long talk with you."

"Suits me down to the ground, Mr. Westabrook," Aunt Save applauded.

In the meantime, the other two members of the Big Eight were running from group to group. Maida Westabrook was saying good-bye to her guests. Dicky Dore, Mrs. Dore's son and Granny Flynn's grandson, alternately lost his mother and found her again. Now he was hugging first his grandmother then his baby sister, Delia.

"Oh, Granny," he pleaded again and again, "how I wish you were coming! Won't you change your mind? Mr. Westabrook says you can at the very last minute if you want to."

"No, my lamb," Granny Flynn declared firmly, her blue eyes sparkling with decision. "I'm too old a body to go traipsing about in camps. I like my comfortable bed. Besides, with Mr. Duncan in the house and Mr. and Mrs. Brine and the Clarks and the Doyles, I'll have as much company as I want. Delia's too young, too, to be camping out."

"I suppose you're right," Dicky declared regretfully.

"Yes, I'm sure she is," announced Maida Westabrook, who entered the room at that moment. "Camping is roughing it, you know, Dicky, and I'd hate to have Granny catch cold or get all tired out."

"I never thought of that," Dicky said remorsefully.

Dicky was Maida's first friend among the Big Eight. It had been a great bond between them that both had been lame. But Maida grew well of her lameness first, and then, through Mr. Westabrook's kindness, Dicky.

Neither of these children looked as though they had been invalids. Dicky was now a tall, strong-looking lad, brown-skinned and brown-haired with limpid, deep eyes and luminous white teeth. Maida was the grey-eyed blonde type. The short, pale gold hair lay close to her head; one moment with a deceptive smoothness, the next ruffling like—

"Do you know, Maida Westabrook," Rosie Brine had said to her once, "your hair is more like feathers than any hair I've ever seen? It looks like the plumage of a bird—if birds were made of gold."

"Her hair's a wonderful color too," added Silva Burle. Silva was the artist of the group. She took great delight in shapes, forms and outlines. She was constantly seeing in things colors that the Big Eight stoutly maintained were not there. "It's a gold with green in it."

"Green hair!" Rosie repeated scathingly. "Yes, Maida—and your lips are purple and your eyes sky-blue-pink."

But perhaps their invalidism had left on Maida and Dicky one trace—a delicate sensitivity which made their faces as mobile as any pond, mirroring every thought and emotion just as the pond registers every flaw and breeze.

"Who ever would have thought, Maida," Dicky exclaimed, "when we first met at Primrose Court, that two years later we'd be going on a camping party in the Adirondacks?"

Marvels had happened in Maida Westabrook's life—marvels of travel, marvels of possession, marvels of friendship. She had toured in the Far West. She had several times visited London and Paris and Rome. Her father had, on one birthday, given her her weight in silver dollars. On another birthday, he had given her a doll house, gigantic for dolls and big, even for children—they could walk about in it. In that, if she chose, she could play all day long with the big family of dolls which had been collected from many countries. On a third birthday, he had given her a little theater, big enough to hold all her friends but small enough to include no grown-ups. She had known the loving devotion of Granny Flynn, her nurse; Dr. Pierce, the family physician;

Bill Potter, a young man, and her father's friend. Yes, she had known all these happy experiences. But from the look in her eyes at this moment, one would have thought that her friendship with Dicky was perhaps the most marvelous thing that had ever happened to her.

"Who would have thought it?" she echoed breathlessly.

CHAPTER IV

THE BIG EIGHT SAY GOOD-BYE

SUDDENLY Mr. Westabrook's stentorian tones rang through the house. "All aboard the lugger," he called. "All aboard for Maida's Little Camp."

Frantic activity manifested itself all over the house. The girls scampered upstairs for their hats and capes. The boys galloped to the New Wing for their caps and coats.

"Wait for me!" came Rosie's agonized accents from above. "Oh, don't leave me behind. I forgot to pack my toothbrush."

Mr. Westabrook, standing in the front doorway, laughed with the rest of the grown-ups who had rapidly gathered about the two beach wagons. "I know just what she did," he explained. "She waited for it to dry before she put it in its little celluloid container."

When the girls came tumbling down the stairs, it was to find that all the grown-ups who lived in the house, all the grown-ups who were visiting in the house and all the Little Seven had gathered to see them off.

Granny Flynn held Delia in her arms. Delia was showing the excitement of departure common to babies, although, this time, she was a little mixed.

"Ev'vybody go away!" she kept calling. "Ev'vybody tum back. Ev'vybody go away *soon.* Ev'vybody tum back *soon.*"

Della held Nesta who, with no very clear idea what all the confusion was about, smiled and crowed and waved her arms. "way . . . tum back . . . way . . . tum back!" she echoed Delia.

Mr. and Mrs. Clark stood with their little twin daughters, Mabel and Dorothy; Mr. and Mrs. Doyle with their two youngest children, Molly and Timmie; Mr. and Mrs. Hale with their youngest child, Betsy.

Mr. Westabrook had discerned that life was rather difficult for all these three families. Mrs. Clark and Mrs. Doyle, faded, tired, patient-looking women, had both married young, had both borne large families of children, who were almost grown when the two younger ones appeared. Mrs. Hale, who was much younger than her husband—all brown like Betsy; pretty and gay like Betsy—had but the one child of her own. But she had become stepmother to a large family of children.

These five children—the Clarks, the Doyles and Betsy—went back to Charlestown for the winter, returned to the Little House for the summer. These long absences eased the financial strain for their families enormously; it gave the tired mothers a chance to rest. Realizing that no one of them ever left the city for more than a day's holiday, Mr. Westabrook was delighted that the three families could rest for all August in the Little House.

Between her father and mother, jumping up and down with excitement, stood Betsy Hale, the pet of the household. "Take me!" she began to call. "Take me, Maida! Take me, Rosie! I'll be a good girl!"

"Take me!" Delia mocked. "Take me . . . good girl."

"Tate me," Nesta followed. "Tate me . . . dood dirl."

The Big Eight were very busy rushing from one to the other, the girls hugging everybody; the boys kissing their parents and shaking hands with the rest.

"You darling," Maida exclaimed, kneeling down to hug Betsy Hale. "How I wish you were going! But I expect we'd take all our time trying to keep you from running away."

Big-eyed and brown-eyed, all tangly, long lashes, big dimples and tiny white teeth, her head running over with curls, Betsy exclaimed, "I never'll run away again—never, never, never!" Even as she spoke, everybody saw her great eyes turn longingly toward the path which led into the woods. Everybody knew that Betsy would forget that promise the instant she was alone.

Mr. Westabrook had taken charge of the packing of the beach wagon. "Zeke, you and Florabelle can start at once with the luggage. I don't know how long this good-bye business is going to last and the sooner you get to the camp the better."

"All right, sir!" Zeke agreed. Florabelle embraced Della and Poppy as though she were going to be gone for years. Poppy's brown eyes even filled with tears at the thought of separation. "Good-bye, Zeke! Good-bye, Florabelle!" everybody called. Zeke helped his wife into the front seat of the first of the two beach wagons and in a moment they were off.

"Now, how about the rest of you?" Mr. Westabrook meditated. "Mrs. Dore and Bunny must sit on the first seat with Robin. But how shall we divide the others?"

"Can't we girls all sit together on one seat?" Maida pleaded.

"Four of you?" Mr. Westabrook asked. "Won't that be a little crowded?"

"Oh, no!" protested Rosie. "It won't be the least bit crowded!" Laura declared. And, "We like to be crowded," Silva put in in her soft voice.

"Then we boys can all sit together on the

seat behind the girls," Arthur suggested.

"But won't that be a pretty tight fit," Mr. Westabrook asked automatically. But before any one of the boys could speak, he added with a twinkle, "I know. Of course, I know. You won't be the least bit crowded. You like to be crowded. All right. Up you go."

Robin Hood took his place on the front seat, back of the wheel, Mr. Westabrook helped Bunny up beside him, then Mrs. Dore. Then one after the other, he assisted the four girls to climb into the seat.

It had been decided that the girls of the Big Eight were to have new traveling costumes. Bunny had designed them. Dark blue slacks with dark blue sweaters; over them, capes that could be easily thrown off; topping all, berets. The first time that Maida had ever seen Rosie Brine, she was wearing a scarlet cape and so Maida begged that Rosie's cape might duplicate that earlier one. Rosie was, in consequence, the most picturesque figure among them. The scarlet cape and beret brought out all the jets in her coloring, but could not deaden its roses. Maida's navy blue cape and beret went well with her blonde tints. The brown of Silva's outfit emphasized her amber hues. Green deepened the pink roses in Laura's cheeks.

The boys wore their boy scout clothes.

Now they were comfortably packed.

"Oh, father," Maida exclaimed suddenly, "how I hate to leave you! But you will come up and see us, won't you?"

"I promise," Mr. Westabrook declared. "I'll pop in on you when you least expect me."

"A month seems an awfully long time," Maida said wistfully.

"Doesn't it," Dicky agreed with her.

"You'll be surprised how quickly that month will go," Mr. Westabrook cheered them. "And when it's over, you won't know which you want most—to keep on staying in camp or to come back home. Are you sure you haven't forgotten anything, Big Eight?"

"Yes," came in chorus from the boys and "Yes," came in chorus from the girls.

"All set, Mrs. Dore?" Mr. Westabrook asked. "All set, Bunny?"

"All set," the two ladies smilingly answered.

"All ready, Robin?" Mr. Westabrook asked.

"All ready," Robin replied.

"Then go," Mr. Westabrook commanded.

Robin Hood put his hands on the wheel. The engine whirred. The beach wagon started forward. Shouts came from the crowd at the door.

"Good-bye!" "Good-bye!" "Good-bye!" "Have a good time!" "Be careful!" "Be a good girl!" "Be a good boy!" "Write often!" "Good-bye!" And out of it all little Betsy's clear little voice, "I'll be a good little girl," Delia's soft cry, "Ev'vybody going away!" and Nesta's "Bye! Bye! Bye!" Everybody waved handkerchiefs in the direction of the beach wagon.

All the Big Eight waved handkerchiefs in the direction of the crowd at the door. "Good-bye!" "Good-bye!" "Good-bye!" "Take care of yourself!" "Yes, we'll write!" "Take care of yourself!"

The beach wagon, gradually achieving speed, followed the drive that, curving across the lawn in front of the Little House, merged with the road leading to the Big House. It turned the corner and was gone.

CHAPTER V

THE BEACH WAGON STARTS

ALTHOUGH the three grown-ups on the front seat maintained a conversation, there was no talk among the Big Eight for a little while. It was as though they were all pondering the fact—and considering it very soberly—that it would be a whole month before they would see their parents again.

Maida, who had always been accustomed to long separations from her father, was the first to throw off this pensive mood. As she was the last to get into the beach wagon, her seat was at the end. She glanced along the three faces. Laura sat next to her, then came Rosie. Their gaze was fixed straight ahead, not seeing, she knew, what they were looking at. On the other end sat Silva. But what was the expression on Silva's face Maida could not say, for Silva had turned her head away.

Maida shifted her position so that she could study the boys' faces. Tyma, sitting at the further end of the seat back of her, was watching the flowing landscape with deep interest. Ah, that was natural enough. Tyma had no home. But Dicky, next to Tyma, and Harold next to Dicky, showed that expressionless mask with which boys try to veil emotion. Arthur just behind her . . . Arthur . . .

A moment, held fascinated, Maida studied Arthur's look.

For Arthur had emerged from the effect of separation from his father and was staring straight ahead at the beautiful August scene. On his face lay a look of an absorption so fierce, of a concentration so hungry, that for an instant the tears pricked Maida's eyes stingingly. Why this was Arthur's first travel! Arthur with all his curiosity about the world, all his reading and studying, all his poring over maps, had probably seen only the two places where he had lived—Charlestown and other parts of Boston, the Little House and adjacent territory. On the other hand, Maida knew that he had roved all over Charlestown and other parts of Boston, during those long days in which he played truant from school. He had seen the Mystic River and the Charles, Boston Harbor, Crescent Beach, South Boston Beach, Nantasket, and Franklin Park. But that was the extent of his traveling experience. And of course, he had played truant at the thrust of that yearning to see new places. Rosie, also—Rosie had enjoyed little holiday visits with relatives who lived about Boston.

But Rosie had never left Massachusetts, had probably never left the county—except to go to the Little House. That was Dicky's story too. The Lathrops were more traveled; they had always summered in Maine. And as for the gypsies, Silva and Tyma—they had lived all over New England.

"How lucky I have been!" Maida thought. "The West once. To Europe three times. I believe I have never thought of that before."

Arthur stirred. "Gee, what pretty country!" he exclaimed.

It was one of those scenes with which Massachusetts abounds, not grand, but pretty and gentle; domesticated and serene; a tiny pond like a plate of silver, with three small, green islands afloat on its surface. Beyond lay fields of high grass, through which a tiny brook meandered to the pond. Beyond all that arose soft hills.

"I'd like to—" Arthur was beginning.

"I'd like to make a map of it," Rosie took it up before Arthur could finish his sentence.

The Big Eight laughed. None of them were as quick as Rosie. But, like her, they realized now that that was what Arthur always felt when he saw a well-defined, interesting stretch of country. He loved to make maps.

"That reminds me," Arthur explained, laughing with the rest of them at the joke on himself. He took a paper from his pocket, unfolded it.

"Well, who'd have ever believed it!" Rosie poked more fun at him. "If it isn't a map! Who'd have ever thought it?"

"Where did you get it, Arthur?" Maida inquired.

"At the garage," answered Arthur. "And I got the route from Robin Hood and marked it in blue pencil here. We go northwest to Fitchburg and then straight across the state of Massachusetts—'like an arrow from a bow,' Robin Hood said. We strike the state of New York just above Albany and then we turn north and keep on going until we bang our heads against a mountain."

"Just think of that!" Rosie exclaimed, "we cross the whole state of Massachusetts."

"We're leaving the ocean behind," Tyma said almost regretfully. "How I shall miss that salt smell in the air."

"But there'll be other lovely smells in the air in the mountains," Maida promised him. "Spicy smells. I love the forest."

"So do I," Silva echoed softly, her joy breaking through the dreams in her expression. "Deep, deep forest—the kind Longfellow meant when he said, 'This is the forest primeval.' "

"Forests full of game," Harold exclaimed. "That's what excites me."

"I can't seem to imagine what real mountains will look like," Rosie declared. "Of course, I've seen pictures—millions of them. But whenever I think of mountains, I don't think of those pictures, I think of the great, white, fleecy clouds you sometimes see in the sky in summer. Oh, I do hope they'll be as beautiful as I expect them to be!"

"They will, Rosie," Maida promised. "More beautiful."

"How many mountain ranges have you seen, Maida?" Arthur asked.

Maida considered. "The Appalachians, the Rockies, the Sierras, the Alps, the Appenines and the Carpathians."

"Gee!" Arthur exclaimed.

"But you've never seen the Adirondacks?" Laura asked.

"No," Maida replied, "never."

"Oh, I'm so glad that you're going to see them for the first time with us," Laura commented in a tone of satisfaction.

An hour more and they were coming into unknown country. They flashed through small villages, separated by lengths of shady tree-lined road, lively, small towns and busy, big cities. They drove for brief periods by tiny brooks purling over stones, for longer ones past wide rivers dropping from dams or sometimes skirted tiny ponds like pewter plates or wide lakes like silver platters. Often the road cut through woodland country and they could gaze into forests so thick and shadowy that as the sunlight, which started pure gold at the tree-tips, sifted downward, it grew paler and dimmer until at the bottom it was almost like an undersea moonlight. All agreed—provided they had believed in fairies—they would expect to find them in these green-shaded spots.

In the little towns they were quick to note the old houses and churches. For the Little House was situated in the heart of Plymouth County and the Big Eight had become accustomed to Colonial architecture. They exclaimed over distinctive features—a fan-lighted door here, windows with twenty-four panes of glass there—Maida could always tell when the glass itself was old—gambrel roofs and overhangs; wells with great well sweeps; charming little summerhouses. And they made intelligent comparison between the steeples of the old, white, wooden churches.

Robin Hood kept drawing their attention to the little Commons which occupied the center of many towns. And Bunny was always calling from the front seat, "Scenery ahead, Big Eight! Don't miss it!"

And then suddenly they were all oh-ing and ah-ing, for they had reached the famous Mohawk Trail and the beginning of the Berkshires—beautiful soft green flutings of hill which rapidly grew higher and rounder until . . .

"The Adirondacks can't be more beautiful than this, Robin Hood," Rosie declared once.

"Perhaps not more beautiful," Robin replied, "but different."

"Higher?" Rosie demanded excitedly.

"Much," Robin Hood answered.

The Trail with its beautiful wide-flung views on both sides, kept them oh-ing and ah-ing. Just before coming into the little town of North Adams which nestles so picturesquely at the end of the Trail, Robin Hood decided to stop for luncheon, for they were all quite ready to eat.

The grown-ups in the Little House had decided that they would save time for what was really a long day's journey, by putting up a luncheon. And Bunny chose to stop at one of those convenient places along the road which, in addition to selling simple hot food, provides rustic tables at which patrons may eat. While Mrs. Dore, Bunny, and the four girls were setting the table with paper tablecloth, napkins, plates and cups, Robin Hood and the boys were bringing, from the diner, bowls of hot soup and pitchers of hot chocolate. Out of the great hamper came hard-boiled eggs, ham and chicken sandwiches, peaches, pears and quantities of Florabelle's delicious cookies.

"I hope Florabelle and Zeke are having as good a luncheon as we are," Maida said as she finished her fourth cooky.

"You may be sure they are," Robin Hood exclaimed. "You see, your father told them to be sure to stop where they could get a chicken dinner. He told Florabelle he wanted her to have a vacation for one meal from her own cooking."

After luncheon, the Big Eight swarmed back into the beach wagon, with undiminished spirits.

"More Massachusetts and more Massachusetts and more Massachusetts!" exclaimed Rosie. "It looks such a little state on the map, but when you come to cross it, it's certainly something. I've never been out of Massachusetts in my life. I'm just dying to get to New York, especially now that we've left the Berkshires behind."

"So am I!" exclaimed Dicky.

"We're in a beautiful part of Massachusetts," Robin Hood called from the front seat. "The western end. It's just as fine in its way as the eastern end."

"I can't wait one minute longer to get to New York," Rosie declared after a long interval of silence. "I don't want to leave this country either." Her voice was full of an amused despair.

"I'm afraid you've got to leave it, Rosie," Robin declared cheerfully. "Read *that!*"

To the right was a double sign. Above appeared the letters *State Line*. Beneath and to the right, was the word Massachusetts with an arrow pointing east. Beneath and to the left, were the words *New York* with an arrow pointing west.

"I never was so excited in my life!" Rosie gasped. "Were you, Arthur?"

"Never," Arthur declared solemnly.

"Farewell my native state!" Rosie flung over her shoulder to Massachusetts. And, "Welcome, New York!" she added.

The Big Eight all laughed.

Of course, for a little while, where one state merged with the other, there seemed to be no difference between Massachusetts and New York. But when, presently, they reached Troy, "Is that the Hudson?" Arthur asked in an awed voice.

"It's the Hudson," Robin Hood answered.

"It's not as big as the Charles," Arthur said in a disappointed voice.

"No, not here," Robin Hood replied. "In Charlestown you see the Charles at its mouth. The Hudson here is not far from its source, but farther south, it swells into one of the widest rivers in the world."

Villages again, small towns, big towns,

cities; brooks, rivulets, rivers; pools, ponds, lakes—the same program manifested itself.

"The houses are all beginning to get different," Maida declared.

"They're squarer and flatter-topped," Laura commented. "And do you notice those little windows up under the roofs with the iron gratings in front of them? Oh, I've noticed so many."

"I have, too," Maida agreed. "That ironwork is beautiful. Some of it is just like lace."

Presently they found themselves traversing a broad valley.

"The Mohawk Valley," Robin Hood informed them.

"Tired, children?" Mrs. Dore asked once.

"Oh, no!" the children chorused. "I wish we could go on forever," Arthur declared fervently.

Nevertheless in the middle of the afternoon there came a sleepy spell. Maida, Rosie, and Laura dozed off for a little while, leaning against each other. Harold and Dicky retired to the back seat where they stretched out for a nap. They left enough place for Tyma to lie down. But Arthur, at one end of the long seat which the boys occupied, and Silva, at the other end of the long seat which the girls occupied, sat spellbound, hungrily drinking in the flashing landscape.

For a while there was complete silence in

the car except for the low-voiced talk on the front seat. Then suddenly, "We're getting into hills again!" Arthur exclaimed. His voice rang like a trumpet, awakening all the sleepers, who sat up rubbing their eyes.

"I wondered when you'd notice that," Robin Hood called. "I've known it for quite a little while. A car always tells you when it starts on an upgrade."

"Does that mean we're getting towards our camp?" Harold asked coming to complete, alert wakefulness.

"Oh, we've got two or three hours yet," Robin Hood said. "You see there will be so much hill-work from now on."

Yes, the land was rising, land rich with forests. Hills that shot up from tender valleys where lay quiet, silver-shining lakes or brawled furious, foaming rivers. Up, up, up they went. Down, down, down they went. Over long stretches of what seemed level road they went. But it was not really level ground, for all the time they were getting higher and higher. Cities disappeared completely. Towns came more and more seldom. Villages appeared at longer and longer intervals.

"We're in *mountains* now," Arthur exclaimed with emphasis finally.

"Yes, you're in the true Adirondacks," Robin Hood assured him.

Farther and farther! Higher and higher!

Brooks tumbling down steep mountain sides. Brooks tearing down mere slopes. Brooks running level by the road. Great forests lifting up to the blue sky. Fine roads with depths of woodland on either side. Flowers. Ferns. Birds. Butterflies. Everything came in for excited comment and eager observation. For now, there came times when, as they rode through valleys, the sun was obscured by mountains.

Arthur looked at his watch. "Six o'clock!" he exclaimed. "We've been up just twelve hours."

Suddenly they turned off the traveled highway on to a dirt road. High trees on both sides. On they went and on. They passed a tiny settlement, a general store which contained the post office, an oil station, two or three nondescript buildings. On they went. The road narrowed a little, grew dustier, began to develop ruts. On and on. Presently Robin Hood turned into a road at the left—a road even more primitive. But here, he drove but for a little space—until suddenly ahead the trees broke. Then he stopped. Arthur flashed to the perpendicular, gazing straight ahead.

"All out! Big Eight!" Robin Hood ordered in an exultant tone.

The children leaped on to the grass. They poured forward, Robin Hood, Bunny and Mrs. Dore leading.

Robin Hood came to that break in the high green wall of the trees. He stopped.

"Welcome to Maida's Little Camp!" he called.

The Big Eight stood stock-still staring.

CHAPTER VI

THE BIG EIGHT ARRIVE

IN BACK, at the west—mountains—retreating far enough away to surround them with forests. In front, to the east—mountains—marching close in a serried formation.

And . . .

Directly in the middle of that spacious front arc, not seeming very far away, dropped a slender, silver thread of waterfall, so fine and misty that it looked as though a high wind must blow it away. The cataract fell into a broad pool at the base of the mountain and there, it produced a thick churning of foamy water which, in turn, threw up a pother of silver mist. Out of the pool emerged a tiny brook which came, all a-bubble, chuckling and singing, straight toward the camp. Before reaching it, however, the tiny stream made an elbow turn, and continued on and out of sight. At that elbow, a tiny rustic bridge crossed it.

The camp itself—that is the house—fitted its location perfectly. Somebody had had the happy idea of building a Swiss chalet among these American mountains. It was a fairly big house of weathered wood. It ran up to a peaked roof and spread out in double, broad and railed piazzas which entirely surrounded it. But the children did not—except for their first cursory glance—look at the house for a long time. Their attention was focused on the scene.

"Oh!" Rosie exclaimed. "A waterfall. A waterfall. I've never seen a waterfall before in all my life."

"And isn't it a beautiful one!" Laura breathed in an awed tone.

"I'm sure I like it better than I'd like Niagara," Silva declared. "It's so slim and frail. It's like lace. It's like a—like a wedding veil."

"It looks something like waterfalls I've seen in the Alps," Maida commented. "But I'm sure it's the most beautiful one I've seen anywhere. Perhaps because it's our own waterfall."

"Think," Rosie said, "of having a *private* waterfall."

In the meantime the boys were quite as voluble as the girls. "Can we climb up the mountain and see where the waterfall starts?" Arthur asked eagerly. And, "Would there be any fish in that brook?" Harold questioned. "How beautiful the two sounds are," Dicky commented acutely, "I wish I could play them both on the piano—the falling water and the running water." "What does the brook run into?" Tyma inquired practically.

"It runs into a lake a mile or two away, Tyma," Robin Hood answered. "There are fish in the brook, Harold. But there's much better fishing in the lake. We'll all try our luck one day. We can climb up to the start of the waterfall, Arthur. I'm afraid I can't help you about those sounds on the piano, Dicky."

Rosie bounced, "Oh, what are we going to do first?" she wailed in pessimistic rapture. "Explore the forest! Climb to the top of the waterfall! Fish in the lake! I shall probably sit like a lump on the piazza all day long just trying to make up my mind."

The Big Eight broke into a babble of excited talk. But before anything could come out of it, the noise of a motor turned all heads about. Zeke and Florabelle were approaching in the other beach wagon.

"Well, you beat me, Mr. Hood," Zeke greeted them. "I got off the road only about twenty miles back and I was some little time finding my way again."

"I should have beaten you, Zeke," Robin Hood declared. "You see I know the road intimately. I've been here many times before. Now boys," Robin Hood addressed the males of the Big Eight, "we're all tired, and the driver is likely to be more tired than anybody else. So I'll ask you to unpack the luggage from Zeke's car."

"I'm not tired, Mr. Hood," Zeke protested.

"My lan'!" Florabelle chimed in, "Ah'm not tired, too. Nobody could get tired after that lovely drive."

Robin Hood smiled, "You'll begin to feel tired pretty soon, Florabelle. Get as simple a supper as possible for the children—only plenty of it."

The boys had already swarmed into the beach wagon, Arthur and Tyma handing suitcases down to Harold and Dicky.

"Could we go in bathing in the brook before supper, Robin Hood?" Arthur asked. "It's been such a hot day," he ended pleadingly.

"I think that's an excellent idea!" Robin Hood declared cheerfully. "You'll find mountain water quite a bit colder than that of the Magic Mirror. At first, you won't want to stay in long. I think I'll take a dip too. Want to go with us, girls?"

"Of course!" the girls chorused.

"And I'm going in too!" Bunny decided.

"All right then," Robin Hood said. "Suitcases in your rooms. Don't stop to unpack. Get into your bathing suits as soon as possible. For when the sun sets, it will get pretty cool here and get cool rapidly."

For several minutes the chalet was filled with the clamor of the boys bumping upstairs with the heavy suitcases. Upstairs consisted of a hall with one long room and one small room on either side. There were five cots in one of the long rooms for Bunny and the four girls; four cots in the opposite chamber for the four boys. Mrs. Dore would occupy the little room at the end of the house at the back, and Robin Hood, its twin, opposite.

But nobody looked at walls or furnishings. Everybody was feverishly opening suitcases, hauling out bathing suits, undressing swiftly and pouring into them. In no time, whatever, the ten of them, Robin Hood in the lead of the boys and Bunny in the lead of the girls, were racing over the soft grass to the water. They all rushed in, dipped and arose screaming hysterically from the delicious exhilaration. The water might have been composed of invisible electric needles so sharp was its instant, chill impact and so tingling its following warmth. The brook was at no place above their knees, but in the middle they lay down and let it pour over them. They churned about industriously for a few minutes.

"I think we've had enough!" Robin Hood declared after a brief interval. "See, the sun's sinking behind the mountains."

"It's balancing right on the edge of the mountain," Rosie declared in a scandalized tone. "It looks just like a plate in spin-the-cover."

They raced to the house, for here and there among them came the sound of chattering teeth. But when they came downstairs at the ringing of the bell, it was to find that Zeke had built a fire in the huge fieldstone fireplace in the center of the back wall of the big living room. Before they sat down to the steaming cream soup which began their simple dinner, they stood bunched in front of the high flames, exclaiming over its warmth.

After dinner, in a suddenly aroused curiosity, the children explored the house. It was all of wood, even the inside walls; no plaster, no paper anywhere. Back of the big room was a wide hall with a stairway leading upstairs; all kinds of big, roomy closets to hold coats, guns, fishing gear and the like.

"This is the gun closet," Robin Hood told them, opening one of the doors. "I shall not bother to lock it, but I don't expect anybody to go into it without my permission."

Back of the hall, side by side, were dining room and kitchen; back of them, storeroom; above, Zeke's and Florabelle's chamber. All the furniture was of wood as simple as possible, except that leather pads softened the wooden seats and that cushions of dark blue denim piled the couches. There were no pictures anywhere. But a fine map of the state hung on one wall and a map of the county on another. There was no bric-a-brac, either, beyond a shelf of . . .

"Some woman has lived here," Silva exclaimed as her eyes fell on the row of flower containers.

"We must fill them with flowers," Maida said, her glance following Silva's.

"I never saw so many doors in my life," Rosie exclaimed. "Every room has at least two doors opening on to the piazza."

"Come here!" Robin Hood called.

He had stepped out on to the piazza. Bunny and all the Big Eight flocked after him. He pointed, at the back, to the west. The sunset glow still quivered, a faint lilac, in the sky and caught in it like a jewel in gauze, glimmered a pale, silver-green crescent moon.

"Oh, how lovely!" Bunny exclaimed. "I never have seen so thin a crescent. It looks as though it were carved out of jade."

"Oh, what a wonderful place!" Rosie exclaimed rapturously. "Waterfalls and crescent moons."

"We'll call the camp Crescent Moon Camp," Maida exclaimed suddenly.

"That's a beautiful name!" Silva approved joyously.

They flocked back to the living room and gathered about the fire; Bunny, the girls, Robin Hood sitting in the big comfortable padded chairs; the boys, cross-legged on the broad hearthstone. They chatted, watching the flying flames.

Bunny, who had been very quiet, suddenly spoke. "I've got to go to bed or else I shall fall fast asleep right here," she declared.

"Sleep!" Laura exclaimed. "I'm sure I could sleep for twenty-four hours."

"Let's try it!" Robin Hood suggested.

CHAPTER VII

THE BIG EIGHT VIEW THE WATERFALL

IT SEEMED that the clangor of the cowbell, which aroused the sleeping camp the next morning, had scarcely ceased before the Big Eight were tearing down the stairs.

"Oh, how I slept," exclaimed Rosie Brine, after the chorus of good mornings had died down. "It was just as though the moment I struck the pillow, I began to sink down, down, down. I felt as though I was falling into a soft, dark—" She paused and meditated.

"Well," Maida supplied.

"No, not a well," Rosie rejected the suggestion.

"Fog?" Laura asked.

"No, not a fog," Rosie rejected this second idea.

"Cloud," Silva put in.

"No," Rosie said with a third definite accent of negation, "not a cloud. It wasn't like any one of those things. I felt as though I was sinking through space forever and ever and ever. It was dark, but oh, so lovely."

"I fancy we all felt that way," Robin Hood said.

"But this air is so wonderful," Silva commented in a soft tone, almost awed. "It's more like something you drink than something you breathe. It's so fresh, yet it's so . . . If an icicle could be air, I'd feel that every time I breathed I was swallowing an icicle."

"I must say that you all show the effects of the mountain air already," Bunny commented. "Instead of displaying one poppy in each cheek, Rosie shows a whole bouquet. Laura's lips are like rubies, and as for you, Silva, and you, Maida, you haven't developed full-blown roses, but you have grown rosebuds."

"Oh!" Maida exclaimed rapturously. "If there's any color in my cheeks, let me see it." She ran across the room and surveyed herself in the mirror which hung over the sideboard.

The three other girls pelted after her. Shamelessly they examined their new beauties, turning their heads first over one shoulder then over the other.

"Tyma," Harold declared in a mincing tone which obviously he hoped was girlish, "your lips are as red as beets. Dicky, your eyes are as big as marbles. And, Arthur, your cheeks are just like red flannel."

"Oh, let me see my lips when they are as red as beets," Tyma exclaimed with a pulsating tremolo.

"Oh, let me see my cheeks when they look like red flannel," Arthur exclaimed in a shrill tenor.

"Oh, let me see my eyes when they look like marbles," Dicky cried in a high falsetto.

The four boys crowded to the other end of the looking glass where they imitated the girls, turning, and twisting.

Everybody laughed, the girls hardest of all. When they sat down to the table to drink their orange juice, to attack the bowls of steaming oatmeal which Zeke placed before them, their mountain-bred spirits kept on rising. After the oatmeal came poached eggs on toast, cocoa, and then for a while, they ate in silence.

While they were in the midst of this last course, Zeke suddenly appeared, tiptoeing through the door which led to the kitchen, his fat forefinger pressed to his lips, his big eyes bulging with excitement. He pointed wordlessly toward the front of the house. Robin Hood leaped noiselessly to his feet, tiptoed over to the window. One glance out and he beckoned to the Big Eight, his finger, in turn, on his lips. In as great a quiet as possible, the children moved to the window.

A pair of deer were drinking at the brook. As they lifted their heads, their horns, complicated as candelabra, drew a graceful design through the morning air. The sunlight quivered so tangibly over their satiny fawn coats that it seemed a liquid—a liquid that would flow down their slender legs and their twitching tails to fall in drops on the ground.

"Oh!" the Big Eight breathed as in one impulse. Over the girls' faces crept the dazed look of the princess in the fairy tale, who wanders into the woods and meets the enchanted stag. But over the boys' faces came a different expression. Harold turned keen and appraising as the sportsman who measures the distance for a shot. Tyma looked pleased, but not surprised, as one who has met this sight before. Arthur and Dicky registered sheer amazement and delight.

The deer drank daintily. They browsed delicately. For several minutes, the group stood frozen at one of the long windows. Then from the kitchen came the crash of a pan which suddenly dropped from Florabelle's excited fingers.

Whirr! Whish! Swish!

With a flit of tails which showed like a flag of derision the white of their undersides, the deer were off. Off through the brook they went and then off over the grassy meadow towards the waterfall in bounds as high and effortless as though the creatures were made of rubber. On and away! Away and on! And now they had reached the woods. And now they were lost to sight.

Maida and Silva stared at the spot where the

deer had disappeared, as though wishing might bring them back.

"Oh," Rosie exclaimed, "I never saw anything so beautiful as that in all my life. How I wish I could leap into the air like a rubber ball!"

Laura ran down the long room bounding at intervals high in the air, as she had been taught at dancing school, her arms and legs shooting out back and front, parallel to each other and to the floor. It was a charming performance. In an ecstasy of rivalry, the boys chinned themselves in the doorway.

"Do you suppose they'll ever come again, Robin Hood?" Silva asked tremulously after a while.

"They may," Robin Hood reassured her, "or others. I hoped we'd see deer on the road coming up. I've seen them there again and again."

"I'm glad," Laura put in, "that our first sight of deer was like this—near Maida's Little Camp. It looked just like a picture in a fairy tale."

The Big Eight chatted about their marvelous experience all during the rest of their interrupted breakfast. After their last mouthful, Robin Hood drew them together into the living room. "Before you go out, I want to talk with you," he said. He motioned to them to sit down. On the center table was one mass of small, irregularly-shaped silvery objects and another of smaller dark, flat, round ones.

"First of all, I'm going to lay down some rules about this camp," Robin Hood began. Suddenly his pleasant voice showed a tone of iron. "These rules are never to be broken. Do you understand that word, *never,* children? And do you understand that when I say never, I don't mean *most of the time.* I mean *never.*"

The Big Eight nodded solemnly.

"Then," Robin Hood went on, his stern voice returning to its easy smoothness, "rule number one. You are, none of you—I mean boys as well as girls—no one of you, nor any group of you, to go into the forest without me until I give you permission. After a while, when I'm sure that you know how to find your way back, I'll let you roam as you will."

He swept the round objects towards him, handed one to each of the Big Eight. "Rule number two. Every morning when you dress, you are to put this in your pocket. It's a compass."

He swept the shining, silvery objects towards him, handed one to each of the Big Eight. "Rule number three. Every morning you are to hang one of these around your neck. They are policemen's whistles. Suppose you have walked too far into the forest and suddenly discover that you're lost. Now comes rule number four. The moment you realize that you're lost, stop walking and stay where you are—I mean by that *exactly where you are.* Don't try to find your way back because the chances are that you'll only get more lost. No, sit down and make yourselves comfortable. But blow the whistle at regular intervals. I assure you that you won't remain lost long. The first part of rule number four is very important—to stop just where you are the moment you feel that you're lost. Do you all understand?"

The Big Eight assented in serious voices.

"Now," Robin Hood permitted in a resigned voice, "you can do what you're all dying to do—try those whistles. Ready!"

For a minute, the air was split with a long, shrill clamor. Zeke, wiping a wet plate, his broad face all one flashing grin, peered into the dining room to see what made the racket.

Robin Hood first put his hands over his ears; then he withdrew one of them, held it up.

Silence fell.

"Now, what would you like to do most this morning?"

Everybody looked at everybody else. "Oh, I'd like to go into the forest," Rosie exclaimed. "I would too," Silva, Laura and Maida agreed. "I'd like to go fishing in that lake you told us about, Robin Hood," Tyma asserted. "I'd like to climb a mountain," Harold declared, "the highest and steepest peak we can find."

"I think I'd like to go into the forest too," Dicky agreed with the girls.

All had spoken except Arthur.

"What would you like, Arthur?" Robin Hood asked him.

"I think I'd like most to wade up the brook to the foot of the waterfall," Arthur suggested a little hesitantly.

There was immediate clamor of approval from the rest of the Big Eight. Every one of them abandoned his pet project immediately.

"Oh, let's go to the waterfall," Rosie echoed rapturously.

"Well, then," Robin Hood decided, "the waterfall, it shall be. I think you'd better all get into your bathing suits. And put on bathing shoes."

There was a swift race up the stairs, a period of milling confusion in the bedrooms and presently the whole party had started off. All except Mrs. Dore, who said that she and Florabelle and Zeke had plenty of work to do in systematizing the camp.

"Oh, how cold this water is," Rosie said. "But somehow I don't feel cold. The sun is so warm."

The sun was warm. It was as though the thin mountain air acted as a burning glass. The sunbeams drove through this burning glass like red-hot lances. Sometimes the Big

Eight were all in the brook and sometimes they were all out of it. Brown stones—they would have been very slippery to their unaccustomed feet if Robin Hood had not suggested wearing bathing shoes—lined the bottom of the brook. Rich ferns grew in plumy greenness close to it. Butterflies fluttered above it. The sun washed the surface of the water with floods of gold except where, occasionally, trees, growing on both sides, met in an arch above. Then the sunlight broke and fell and floated on the surface of the water like hundreds of golden coins too light to sink.

"It's much farther than I thought it was," Rosie said in an astonished tone. "I didn't think it would take us more than ten minutes to get there."

"Mountain air is so much thinner than the air you're accustomed to, Rosie," Robin Hood warned her, "that everything will seem much nearer to you than it really is. It will take us all of half an hour to get to the pool."

It took much more than a half an hour, for they were stopping every moment to look at things.

"It's all so different from home," Rosie grumbled once, "and I can't exactly see how it's different. We have trees near the Little House and a pond. There are brooks on Mr. Westabrook's place. But they don't look like these and I can't exactly say what makes the difference."

"For one thing, the trees are taller," Arthur said.

"Yes," Robin Hood agreed, "that's one difference. And we're much higher here, you know. Altitude makes continuous changes until—if you get high enough—you come into a new country or a different zone."

"Oh, look!" Dicky breathed suddenly.

Out of a covert at one side flashed an orange blur. It streaked across the green, disappeared into deeper forest.

"Oh! Oh! Oh!" the Big Eight cried.

"A fox!" Rosie exclaimed jubilantly. "Just think of it, a fox! Of course, I've read about foxes, but I've never been any nearer to one than that one in the fable, *The Fox and the Grapes.* Yet I knew it was a fox the instant I looked at it."

"What a country," Arthur gasped. "What other animals could we possibly see, Robin Hood?"

"You've already seen white-tailed deer and a red fox," Robin Hood answered the question. "There are grey foxes as well as red, and grey squirrels as well as red. You might see raccoon, mink, otter, marten, fisher and oppossum. You might, if you're lucky, run across a wildcat and if you are luckier still—that is if you'd *like* to see him—his cousin, the Canadian lynx. Also there's the varying hare or snow-shoe rabbit. He's rather interesting because in the winter, he changes his coat from grey to white and grows a large number of thick hairs on his feet, so that he can run on top of the snow. Of course—although this is the most unlikely thing in the world—you might see a bear."

"A *bear!*" Arthur exclaimed. "Oh, how I'd love to see a bear."

"Well, I *wouldn't,*" Rosie said with emphasis.

"I like bears," Maida said. "Berne, in Switzerland, has a bear in its coat-of-arms and you can buy bears carved in wood everywhere there from little bits of cubs not more than an inch or two long, to great big creatures taller than a man. And in Berne they have a bear pit with lots of real live bears in it."

"What do you mean—lots?" Arthur asked.

"I don't mean lots," Maida corrected herself, "I mean several. The pit is divided in the middle," Maida explained, "and I should say there are perhaps four in each compartment. You can buy carrots nearby—bears love carrots you know—to feed them with. It's the most amazing thing the way the bears act when they see you dangling the carrots. Sometimes, they dance a long dance sideways—oh, such a grotesque dance—to get you to throw them down. They join their paws as though they were praying and put them first on one side of their face and then on the other. The funny thing about it is that nobody teaches them these tricks. Somebody must have taught the first bears generations ago. All the younger ones that have come since, have copied them from the older generation. I used to walk down to the bear pit every single day."

"I should like a bear very much," Rosie agreed satirically, "if he was in a pit and there was an iron railing between him and me. But to meet him in the forest—*no thank you!*"

"I don't think you'll have to worry about that, Rosie," Robin Hood reassured her. "I've never seen hide nor hair of one in all my exploration of the Adirondacks."

"What kind of bear are there in New York?" Arthur asked.

"The black bear," Robin Hood answered. "At growth, they weigh about two hundred and fifty pounds."

"I love bear cubs," Laura said, "I've seen them in the circus."

"Bear cubs," Robin Hood explained, "or at least this New York variety, are full of play. They're very gentle. They make nice pets. Ah, here we are."

"Here" was the pond. The crowd of children, all bunched together, rushed forward, stepped within the circumference of the pretty sheet of water. Rosie was first. It was deeper than she expected. She slipped. Her hand, reaching out, seized Maida. Maida slipped. Involuntarily, Maida clutched Silva. Silva grabbed Tyma. Tyma caught Arthur. Laura, Dicky and Harold were carried in in the rush and all the Big Eight disappeared under the water. They bobbed up at once much surprised and very breathless, but quite ready to join in Bunny's and Robin Hood's laughter.

Presently they crossed the pretty pool and stood round in an admiring group, looking up at the delicate film of waterfall.

CHAPTER VIII

THE BIG EIGHT EXPLORE THE FOREST

THERE was no discussion at luncheon as to what the Big Eight would do that afternoon, for they were all in accord. Having spent the morning trailing through water, they wanted to spend the afternoon exploring the woods. And so, after Robin Hood had smoked his post-luncheon pipe, they started off. But in the meantime, sitting on the piazza with the children grouped about him, he gave them a little talk.

"Now," he began, "you all have your compasses with you, so there's no reason why you shouldn't know in what direction we're heading. But some of you—Silva, for the girls, and Arthur and Tyma for the boys—can calculate pretty well in what direction you're going from the position of the sun. I want you all to learn to do that. You've had some elementary lessons in woodcraft too. You know how to start a fire—even when it rains. And I am sure I've dinged it into you that you must never leave a fire without being sure it's completely out. But you've never had any experience with such woods as you're going to see now. And I want you all to use your eyes as you've never used them before. You will find blazes on the trees here and there. By *blaze*s I mean a spot where somebody has notched a tree with an axe. But I want you to blaze your own trails. In other words, I want you to note rocks, trees, clumps of bushes—noticeable marks of every kind—so that you will recognize them again. It may be that, when we have got a little distance from the camp, I'll turn you all loose to see if you can find your way back. How would you like that?"

He looked about at the circle of interested faces. Laura's face wore a serious questioning look; Maida gazed abstractedly forward.

"I'm a little frightened at the thought," Laura admitted bravely.

"So am I," Maida declared.

"You needn't do it unless you want," Robin Hood reassured them hastily. "There'll be plenty of these experiments. And this first time, I'll send you in pairs."

"Oh, if I can go with Maida!" Laura exclaimed.

"Oh, if I can go with Laura!" Maida exclaimed.

Robin Hood knocked the ashes out of his pipe, put his pipe into his pocket. "Let's go!" he suggested. "Let's try the forest at the back. First of all, though, see if you can find a trail."

The Big Eight ran back and forth at the edge of the forest, studying it carefully.

"Oh, I think I've found it!" Laura called after a few minutes.

"You have," Robin Hood reassured her. "That's it! Good for you, Laura!"

The Big Eight raced in Laura's direction, the boys obviously chagrined at Laura's cleverness.

There was a trail, but a very faint one. "It isn't much like the trails on Spectacles Island," Dicky said.

"Nor will you find these woods like those on Spectacles Island," Robin Hood warned him. "Nor those on Mr. Westabrook's estate. Mr. Westabrook's woods have been forested with the utmost care, the paths kept clear. But here nature has had her own way—as you will find presently."

They entered the trail in Indian file.

"Laura," Robin Hood suggested, "you found the trail, so suppose you go first. When you lose it, we'll let whoever finds it take the lead."

It was amazing by what swift degrees this new green world caught and surrounded them. Trees seemed to slip quietly in back of the Big Eight and then to gather into close towering companies. Bushes seemed to move forward in front and to ring them with impregnable walls of green. Presently they might have been prisoners, wandering through a green maze.

"Why you can't see anything of the camp," Maida exclaimed suddenly. "I almost feel as if we were lost." There was, for an instant, a note of panic in her voice.

"But what magnificent trees," Robin Hood exclaimed instantly. "Let's all stand still for a moment and look up at them."

"Oh!" Maida said in an awed tone after a moment of observation, "I never saw such trees in my life."

Great beeches spired like church steeples. Great oaks towered like medieval castles. Great maples spread like gigantic beehives. Enormous pines—cones caught among the iridescent needles—gloomed. Verdant birch, pearly aspen, silvery poplar fluttered and sparkled. Firs—there were many of these—lifted velvety, green triangles here and there.

"What masts those beeches would make!" Tyma exclaimed. "Gee, I wish there were clipper ships nowadays, so there could be masts and great sails."

"What a Christmas tree that fir tree would make," Rosie said. "We'd have to have a fireman's ladder to trim it and it would take miles of glittery stuff and millions of Christmas tree ornaments to cover it."

The momentary look of panic had fled from Maida's face. A look of exaltation had taken its place. "Oh, how beautiful it would be, Rosie, to have a Christmas tree in the forest!"

"Are you all watching," Robin Hood warned them, "for sign-posts—trail-posts—to show you your way back?"

"I am," Arthur answered. "I noticed a maple with one branch that had turned red and—"

"Oh, I noticed that!" Rosie exclaimed. "And I noticed an oak tree with a great round wart at the side."

"I noticed that," Tyma agreed eagerly. "And a fat rock, shaped like the shell of a Big Bertha."

"I saw that too," Harold broke in. "And a great clump of white birch—I counted eleven of them."

"And a tiny opening where ferns were growing," Silva added.

"And I saw the ashes of some camper's fire," Dicky concluded.

"You've done very well," Robin Hood praised them. "Now let's go on. Take the lead, Laura."

"I've lost the trail," Laura admitted shamefaced. "I don't think I would have if we hadn't stopped, but now I'm all confused."

"That's perfectly natural, Laura," Robin Hood reassured her. "You've done remarkably well. Now let's see who finds the trail first."

The Big Eight scattered, leaving Bunny and Robin Hood alone.

"I've found it!" Arthur exclaimed triumphantly.

Everybody hurried to the spot where he stood. It was true that Arthur had found it. And so, for the time being, he became chief of the safari. It was obvious that he was determined not to lose his advantage, for—as he advanced—he studied every aspect of the scene in front of him. Once or twice he paused, but always he went on. And all the time, the green world kept closing, fold after fold, behind them.

Suddenly Robin Hood called a halt. "Now," he said, "we've been going half an hour—"

"Half an hour!" Bunny exclaimed. "I would say that we'd been walking an hour. Not that I'm tired but that I've seen so many trees."

"Now," Robin Hood said, "I'm going to turn you loose. See if you can retrace your steps. Remember, the instant you're not sure where you're going, blow the whistle once. I'll answer with my whistle. You answer with yours. Keep answering me and I'll find you in two shakes of a lamb's tail. When you get to the edge of the camp, whistle twice, close together. You understand—I'll know by the two whistles when you've got home. Now, is there any one of you who doesn't want to try this game today?"

"I think I won't," Bunny said instantly. "I'll stay with you, Robin Hood."

"All right, then," Robin Hood declared, "I'll send you off one at a time. You start first, Tyma. In the meantime, don't forget your trail-posts."

Tyma started off with the swiftness of a homing dove. They realized how leisurely had been their pace when in a surprisingly brief time, they heard two whistles—a little faint, to be sure, but much louder than any one of the Big Eight would have expected them to be.

"Tyma's in camp," Robin Hood said. "Now you, Rosie. Are you sure you want to attempt it?"

"I wouldn't miss it for anything on earth," Rosie declared. She, too, started like a bullet from a gun and made off in the direction Tyma had taken. Presently sounded two whistles again.

"Rosie's safe," Robin Hood smiled. "Now, Arthur."

Arthur started off with as confident an air and with the same swiftness that Tyma and Rosie had shown. They could hear his footsteps for a while. Then they stopped. Then they heard crashings among the bushes. There came a pause. Followed a single whistle.

"Arthur's lost," Robin Hood explained.

"Don't move from here. I'll find him in a moment."

Robin Hood whistled. Arthur answered. Robin Hood dove into the trees. Immediately, after he had disappeared, Robin Hood whistled again and Arthur answered again. In a brief time Robin Hood was back, Arthur behind him.

"I deserve it all," Arthur explained. "Smarty-cat! I was so crazy to keep my position at the head of the line, finding that trail, that I completely forgot to look out for trail-posts. It's a great joke on me."

"It's an excellent lesson," Robin Hood agreed. "I did that two or three times before I learned better. Your turn, Harold."

Harold's two whistles followed in a brief time. Then Laura took the trail. Then Dicky. Then Maida. All four arrived safely. But Silva, like Arthur, came to grief. Passing the little green dell, filled with ferns, she was tempted to enter it. The beautiful ferns proved to be so great a distraction that she wandered a pace or two to gather a bouquet. When she came to return to the trail, she could not find it. After a while she blew her whistle and Robin Hood came to her rescue.

When the remaining quartette, Bunny and Silva, Robin Hood and Arthur, emerged from the forest, they found the triumphant road-finders of the Big Eight all climbing trees. Rosie had, of course, gone higher than anyone else. Her scarlet beret gleamed like some strange tropical fruit from a high branch.

"Come down now, children," Robin Hood called in his easy tones. "Do you know how long we've been in the forest? About three hours. I think you'd better be getting ready for dinner."

CHAPTER IX

THE BIG EIGHT CLIMB—A MOUNTAIN?

"BIG EIGHT," Robin Hood asked the next morning, "what shall we do today?"

The Big Eight answered with its usual clamor. Robin Hood's hands went to his ears, but when silence ensued, he took them away. "I'll tell you what I caught out of all that noise," he said smilingly. " 'Climb the mountain.' 'Go fishing.' 'Find the top of the waterfall.' 'Explore the forest again.' Now I propose that we do one hard thing this morning, then one rather easy thing this afternoon. Suppose we go to the top of the waterfall now. I think I'd rather wait a little longer before we attack a mountain—until you've found your mountain legs. Besides it will take most of a day. We'll eat our lunch on the mountain top. This afternoon we can go fishing."

"Oh, I'm so glad we're going fishing," Harold said with satisfaction. "I've been dying to get to that lake ever since we got here."

"Bathing suits, Robin Hood?" Arthur asked.

"No, I think not. We may find it cool above

the waterfall. And you can all go in bathing when we get back."

"That's nice," Arthur agreed, "because then we're all ready."

They were all ready and again with Bunny and Robin Hood in the van, they started off. They took the little bridge, crossed the grassy meadow and struck off to the edge of the forest.

"You seem to know just where to go, Robin Hood," Harold commented.

"Oh, I've climbed to the top of the waterfall several times," Robin Hood explained.

"Then you've been here more than once, Robin Hood," Maida commented in a surprised tone.

"Yes," Robin Hood agreed. "I knew the people who built this camp. Just after I came out of Harvard, I spent a whole summer here. I've explored this whole country. My friends wanted a wilder scene so they moved west. But when Mr. Westabrook spoke of a camp in the Adirondacks, I suggested this."

"I think of the mountains every night in bed," Rosie said, "and then I feel that I want to climb every one of them to see what's on the other side."

"If we could only fly," Silva sighed. "I mean if we had wings just as we have skates. If we could only go to the hall closet, take down our wings from the hook where they're hanging, throw them over our shoulders, fasten them under our arms, then step out into the air, spread our wings and go as high as we wanted. Oh, how I should love that! To fly over trees and lakes and mountains and straight through clouds!"

"I quite agree with you, Silva," Robin Hood said sympathetically. "That would be the perfect way to do a great deal of our traveling. To see a mountain from the air first. Then to climb it. Then to see it from the air again. That would be prime. Perhaps we'll do that some day."

Talking and laughing, they approached the trees which bordered thickly the pebbly meadow they were traversing. Soon they saw that a trail opened just ahead. Involuntarily everybody hurried a little. Robin Hood and Bunny let the Big Eight pass them.

"I'll let them race as fast as they want to now," Robin Hood said in an undertone to Bunny, "they'll need all the breath they've got later."

Once under the shade of the trees, the Big Eight began to meet again those features of the forest which always gave them pause. A tree so tall that they gathered in a circle about it, staring up to the top. A great lichened rock which they circumnavigated. A bed of ferns, like crowded triangles of green lace. A stretch of moss, softer than any velvet to the foot. The gurgle of water . . .

That sound was an invitation that no one of them could ever refuse. In a minute they would be on their knees, drinking, from their cupped hands, the cold, delicious water which flowed by the trail.

"It isn't like any water that I ever tasted," Laura exclaimed ecstatically. "And how wonderful that it's so cold."

Back and forth, the children flitted, forth and back. Robin Hood and Bunny, talking busily, kept to their even pace. Occasionally one of the Big Eight would bring a leaf for Robin Hood to identify, a flower.

Laura had a quick eye for leaves. "I know what I'm going to do," she cried suddenly, "I'm going to make a collection of leaves. I noticed that you've brought up some big blank-books, Robin Hood. Could I use one of them to press my leaves in? I want to bring it back to Mr. Westabrook."

"That was the object back of bringing up the books," Robin Hood declared promptly. "I think it would be an excellent idea, Laura. You've no idea how quickly you learn trees, shrubs, vines and flowers—if you collect the leaves."

"I'll show you how to put them into the book, Laura,".Bunny offered.

"I'm ashamed I didn't think of that myself, Laura," Maida said. "I think I'll press flowers in a book for father."

"I'll have to collect something for him too," Silva exclaimed, knitting her brows.

"I should too," Rosie agreed. "I'll tell you what we'll do, Silva. You collect rocks and I'll collect trees."

"How would you like to knit Mr. Westabrook a pair of stockings, Rosie?" Bunny asked. "I brought plenty of worsted and knitting needles with me. I'll teach you to knit in no time."

"I'd love it," Rosie exclaimed.

"How about you, Silva?" Bunny asked.

"I'd like to learn to knit," Silva answered, "but I want to paint something special for Mr. Westabrook—I don't quite know what yet. But don't bother, Bunny darling. I'll think of it."

The trail wound enough for the Big Eight not to realize for some time that they were climbing a slope. But gradually, the flights among the great trees on both sides of the trail ceased.

"Goodness!" Rosie exclaimed once. "This isn't such easy going as it was."

"No," Robin Hood agreed quizzically. "Mountain climbing is likely to become hard going. But remember this is not real mountain climbing. This is a very small, comfortable, domestic little slope."

Harold, who was always in the van of this exploration, called back, "Oh, I'd like to do some regular climbing over snow-covered mountains with glaciers and great crevasses and avalanches. Climbers all tied together, cutting steps for themselves out of the ice."

"Not for me, thank you!" Rosie exclaimed. "I'd fall over the very first cliff. Once I went up Bunker Hill Monument in Charlestown—two hundred and twenty-five feet—and when I got to the top, I didn't know which was most frightening—to stay there and look out over the country or come down. Heights make me dizzy."

"Have you done any of that kind of mountain-climbing?" Arthur asked Robin Hood.

"Not much—a little," he replied. "I'm not so interested in work among snow and ice. The tropics thrill me much more than the Arctic or the Antarctic."

Now the trail was getting steeper. Small stones turned and rolled downwards under the eager attack of the Big Eight.

"Watch your step!" Robin Hood urged. "I wouldn't like to have anyone sprain an ankle here. That would mean that you would be laid up for most of the month."

The eight young faces frowned at this suggestion. For a few minutes they all walked as though they were treading on eggs. But gradually their confidence returned, although obviously that phrase "would be laid up for most of the month" had sunk deep into their minds.

"I think the trees are a little thinner now," Arthur observed once.

"Perhaps," Robin Hood agreed, smiling.

"And they're not quite as high or as big," Tyma observed.

"Perhaps," Robin Hood smiled again.

"Oh, I hear water," Dicky exclaimed. "I wonder how far away it is."

"I think we'd better keep to the trail now," Robin Hood suggested. "You might have to do quite a bit of climbing before we find that brook."

Arthur was looking off towards the right. Then suddenly he turned his head. "I hear more water over to the left," he declared.

"What a lovely sound running water makes!" said Dicky. "How I wish I could write a symphony of many waters—showers and great storms; tides and oceans; waves and brooks and rivers and waterfalls."

"What a lovely idea," Bunny exclaimed. "How I wish you could. Have you ever tried to write any music, Dicky?"

"No," Dicky answered dolefully, "I don't believe I could. I wish I might, though."

"Perhaps you will some day," Bunny encouraged him. "That's the way I used to feel about writing. Even when I was a little girl, I wanted to write books. I made up my mind that I was going to do it and somehow I did. But I did it because I kept it in my mind all the time. Now you hold it in your mind that you want to write music. And keep experimenting at the piano and see if you can't make some sounds that seem to you to represent all those things—ocean waves, brooks and cascades."

"I certainly will try," Dicky declared.

"How many fallen trees we've seen!" Maida exclaimed dreamily. "What makes a tree fall, Robin Hood? Their roots look so long and thick and heavy, you'd think they would hold tight long after the tree was dead."

"You see, Maida," Robin Hood explained, "as a tree dies it molders all along its length. And then sometimes the break comes and it falls in perfectly calm weather. But often a wind helps. The old roots aren't strong enough to hold it. So over it goes!"

"Father and I saw so many dead trees in the Rockies and the Sierras," Maida told them. "Father said that some places looked as though a group of great giants were just about to start a game of jackstraws. He said it was so different in the Alps. The Swiss people use every bit of fallen wood for kindling. The Alps were as clean as though every day an army of giant housemaids went through them with carpet sweepers and vacuum cleaners and dustpans and brushes and dustcloths. Why, father used to say that there was enough fallen timber in the Rockies to keep the whole world warm for years. And such great bunches of trees and branches caught among the rocks in the mountain rivers everywhere."

"A fallen tree is very beautiful, I think," Bunny said. "I always have a feeling that I'd like to sketch it—it's so mossy and soft."

After this little jet of conversation, silence fell for a while, for now they were approaching an open space.

"That water is getting louder and louder," Dicky declared. "Oh, I know what it is," he said in an amused voice, "it's the waterfall."

At these magic words everybody tried to hurry but nobody could—the way was too steep. But the singing of the waterfall grew louder and louder. The last steep step brought them on to a broad platform of rock, cleft by a narrow, brawling stream. The stream, clear as glass, flooding past ferns and grasses and just as it dropped, throwing up a gossamer mist, poured over the side of the mountain.

"What a scene!" Bunny gasped. But with the Big Eight she threw herself on the ground and rested for a while.

Up into the ether—everywhere bubbled mountains. Mountains so covered with trees that, in the distance, they took on a velvety softness. Mountains so crisscrossed with streams that, in the distance, they looked as though they were basted with silver threads. Below lay the upland meadow, which they had traversed, to get to the foot of the mountain, the little brook with its single bridge looking like a toy in a miniature Japanese village, and beyond, the chalet. Even as they stared, Zeke came out of the house, then returned again.

"Oh, there's that lake you spoke of, Robin Hood," Harold said eagerly. "Isn't it pretty!"

"Look, Big Eight," Robin Hood said, pointing off to the west. "See, there's a shower."

Off in the distance, a dark huddle of slim, straight darts showed against a silvery-grey sky.

"A shower," Rosie said in an awed tone. "I never dreamed that I could see a shower, all separate by itself, in the distance."

"How close the clouds look to the mountain tops way off," Silva said. "As though, if you were standing there, you could reach up and pull them down about you. But I suppose they wouldn't seem near at all if you were right under them."

"No nearer than they do here," Robin Hood explained.

The children stared up at the white cloud above them as though they were trying to measure the distance. They sat there for a long while talking, pointing out cloud changes, to each other, watching cloud shadows race across the world, counting mountains and trying to discover new rivers and lakes. Presently, Robin Hood said, "I think we'd better be starting now. That will give us about time to get home for luncheon."

"That luncheon will taste very good," Maida commented pensively.

An enthusiastic murmur of approval came from the Big Eight.

It was surprising how much more quickly they came down than they went up.

"How high did we go, Robin Hood?" Arthur asked.

"About a hundred feet," Robin Hood admitted, grinning.

"Well, that's not mountain-climbing," Arthur exclaimed in disappointment. "And I thought," he added in a self-accusal, boyishly bitter, "that the trees were growing thinner."

"And I said," Tyma declared in a twin access of self-contempt, "that they were getting smaller."

"I didn't correct you," Robin Hood explained, "because I wanted you to find your mistake for yourself. I thought it would teach you how easy it is to believe what we want to believe. It's partly my fault. I deliberately took you by the longest trail so as to confuse you. But maybe in a few days we'll take a real climb and then you'll see a little difference perhaps between the trees at the top and those at the bottom. Remember though that these are low mountains."

"I can't wait for it," Arthur declared in a low tone. "And as for Harold—he's almost fit to be tied, waiting so long."

Arthur paused and then he smiled. "But after all," he added, "even Harold will have to admit that a few days is not a century."

CHAPTER X

THE WEATHER CHANGES

BUT Dame Nature stepped in that afternoon to change the plans of the Big Eight.

"It's getting dark," Maida exclaimed in the midst of luncheon.

"I've been noticing that," Arthur admitted. "But I hoped if I said nothing about it, the sun would come out."

Bunny smiled and Robin Hood smiled. "It may be only one of those mountain showers," Robin Hood remarked. "It may last only a few minutes."

"I hope so," Bunny said buoyantly. "I want to go fishing just as much as Harold does."

It turned out at first to be a mountain shower. Thunder like the proverbial giants' game of nine-pins rolled in the hills. Lightning zigzagged in a kind of skyey geometry, splendid but insane. Then thunder and lightning ceased. It settled into a steady hard rain.

"No fishing today, I'm afraid," Robin Hood decided firmly.

"Well, there are a lot of things we all ought to do," Rosie declared philosophically. "We really haven't settled ourselves in shipshape style yet and I think we all ought to write to our parents. And I think we all ought to write a letter to Mr. Westabrook."

"You're very thoughtful, Rosie," Bunny said. "I had made up my mind that you would have to settle yourselves down to it tomorrow morning anyway. But as long as this rain has come, let's all do it now. Suppose you go upstairs and put everything to rights there. Then if you come down here, we'll write a round robin letter to Mr. Westabrook."

An hour of concentrated labor followed. Clothes that had only been hung up hastily on hooks in closets, found themselves transferred to hangers. Hats and caps ranged along closet shelves in immaculate order. Shoes that had piled into higgledy-piggledy masses on the floor found themselves straightened into files, fairly military. Stockings sorted themselves into trim rows. Ties hung themselves neatly over hooks. After a while the confusion of footsteps died down in the boys' rooms as its occupants came clattering down the stairs.

"I wonder why it is," Arthur said to Bunny, "that it always takes girls longer to do anything that is connected with clothes than boys. It always takes them longer to dress or to pack or to unpack. I never could understand it."

Bunny smiled sympathetically. "That's a question that some men ask themselves all their lives, Arthur," she explained. "But those men are not observant—or at least not sympathetically so. If you give the matter the kind of study that you would give to the habits of a strange bird or a new animal, you'd soon find out the reason. First of all, girls' clothes require a great deal more care in packing than boys' do. You see, you don't have ruffles and tucks and laces to consider. Girls have. And then there's a quality about most girls which is very desirable in them, but is not demanded of men. That is daintiness. Girls like to be dainty. That involves wrapping things in tissue paper or packing them in separate boxes. Do you understand, Arthur?"

"I do now," Arthur said. And then after an interval of thought, he added a remark which showed a kind of wisdom for a boy of his age, "There always seems to be a good reason for almost anything, doesn't there—I mean if you study it long enough."

"Arthur," Bunny exclaimed earnestly, "if you've learned that now—oh, I can't tell you how much difficulty that knowledge will save you. All your life, you will have an understanding spirit if you keep saying to yourself, 'There's probably a good reason for it.' "

The girls came pouring down the stairs.

"I know what you've been doing," Arthur accused them "you've been being dainty."

"Been being dainty!" Rosie repeated in a

mystified tone. "Have you gone crazy, Arthur?"

"Oh, no, Rosie," Bunny explained, "it's only a little talk we've had. Arthur wanted to know why it took girls so much longer than boys to pack and unpack and I told him that girls were dainty about it."

Bunny had brought pens and ink into the living room, had placed them on big blotters. A pile of notepaper and envelopes and a sheet of stamps occupied the center of the table.

"I, also, was just as dainty as I could be," Dicky asserted.

Everybody laughed, but nobody asked Dicky for proof.

"I put my toothbrush in a glass tube," Dicky boasted proudly.

"Let's write our letter to Mr. Westabrook first," Bunny suggested. "Then you can take your own time about writing to mothers and fathers."

"I was thinking about the letter to Mr. Westabrook while I was upstairs," Rosie suggested. "Mr. Westabrook always enjoys our jokes on him, and so I thought we might play another little joke. Of course, there's everything in the world up here that anybody could want, a river, a pool, a lake, a waterfall, forests and mountains. I thought we might complain in the first note because there were no glaciers, or volcanoes, or geysers, or—"

"Deserts," Laura suggested.

"All right," Robin Hood agreed, "if it's going to be a joke, I'll let you write your own letter. But remember always that a joke must be done very—very—"

"Delicately," Bunny supplied the word for him.

"*Daintily,*" Dicky insisted. "Let me write it. Remember that toothbrush."

"Exactly," Robin Hood received Bunny's suggestion, "delicately—or else it becomes just plain rude. Now, Bunny, suppose you and I go out into the dining room and let this crowd make up their own letter. We'll wait until you tell us you've finished it."

Bunny and Robin Hood retired. They could hear a steady hum of conversation in the front room, followed by a silence, in which apparently, the Big Eight were watching somebody write. Often there came a brief, high-voiced argument. Then laughter. Silence. Talk again. Presently Arthur came to the door, "We've finished the letter," he exclaimed triumphantly. "You read it, Maida."

Maida, holding a much blotted sheet of letter paper, dutifully read:

Jerome Westabrook, Esq.
Big House
Satuit
Massachusetts

Dear Mr. Westabrook:

The undersigned, Big Eight have been settled in Maida's Little Camp for nearly three days. They have explored the neighborhood with a great deal of interest and they announce regretfully that they have found no:

Deserts
Quicksands
Icebergs
Glaciers
Geysers
Hot springs
Volcanoes

They wish to say that it doesn't make any difference whatever that there are none of those things at Maida's Little Camp. It seems to them that we never had a better time—no, not even on Maida's Little Island. They know we can't stay here forever but we wish they could. They would like Maida's Little Camp to be tacked onto Maida's Little House so that we could go back and forth. We feel so happy and so grateful that they do not know how to thank you. But if you will only come up to visit us as soon as ever you can, they'll tell you all that we do not know how to write.

Laura
Rosie
Silva
Maida
Dicky
Tyma
Harold
Arthur

"I think that's a very nice letter," Bunny commented.

"So do I," Robin Hood agreed. "I know it will please Mr. Westabrook."

The rain kept up and an early darkness set in. The boys built a fire and after the Big Eight had finished their letters, they gathered about it.

"How would you like me to read you the story of Rip Van Winkle, Big Eight?" Bunny asked. "You see Rip Van Winkle was a New York man and all the strange things that happened to him, happened in this state."

"Oh, I'd love it!" Silva cried.

Bunny had tucked Washington Irving's *Sketch Book* into her suitcase. Maida ran upstairs and brought it down. The children listened spellbound while Bunny read the story.

Rain still poured. After dinner, when the Big Eight filed into the living room, they found the center table heaped with the pieces of a jigsaw puzzle.

"It's the United States," Bunny told them. "Let's see how soon you can put it together."

Of course, they all thought that they would put it together in no time. But it was a very big puzzle and many of the pieces were small and some quite baffling in their irregularity. Beside the Big Eight discovered that their geography was lamentably weak.

"Oh dear me, where is Idaho?" Rosie moaned.

"And there are two Norths and Souths, aren't there?" Tyma complained. "Carolinas and Dakotas."

The clock struck nine soon after they had finished it. They were all yawning. They did not say they were glad to go to bed, but it was obvious that they could not keep their eyes open a moment longer.

The next morning the Big Eight awoke into a world which still whirled with rain. The mountains at the back had almost disappeared. Those in front looked like weak, undefined photographs of themselves. Only the waterfall was fairly clear—a white streak, parting darkness.

The Big Eight actually lingered as long as they could over the work allotted to them. The boys volunteered to chop wood for kindling and the girls to cook custards and cake for dinner. Rosie made a big sheet of her famous fudge. But even all this could not keep their eagerness long at work. They worked out another jigsaw puzzle.

Immediately after luncheon, Robin Hood said, "How many of you would like to take a walk in the rain?"

A delighted hubbub greeted this suggestion.

"All right, then," Robin Hood agreed, "rubber boots, rubber coats and tarpaulins."

"We look like a mob of firemen," Harold commented later as the ten dark, glossy figures emerged from the chalet into the rain.

They ventured for a little distance into the forest. But there, it was so dark as to be decidedly gloomy. When Robin Hood said, "How would you like to walk down to the lake?" there was an immediate and enthusiastic assent.

They retraced their steps through the woods and over to the brook. The brook seemed as gay as ever; the rain could not flatten its bubbling, nor deafen its song. The Big Eight tramped along squashily for more than a mile. Presently, they saw ahead a wide sheet of water which might have been of lead, so grey was the light that revealed it.

It was a fairly big lake. Surrounded by trees, high sedges growing in spots near the shore, it was the biggest expanse of fresh water that the Big Eight had ever seen so close at hand.

"Won't it be beautiful when the sun shines on it," Bunny exclaimed.

They splashed back through the wet very gay and talkative, as though with a sense of unspent treasure.

It was getting dark when they arrived at the chalet. Mr. Westabrook had, as far as dress was concerned, laid but one rule on the Big Eight. And that was that they were to put on fresh clothes for dinner. That changing had become a habit and now they filed up to their rooms as a matter of course. The upstairs resounded with the splashing of water in the showers and the pouring of water from pitchers into bowls. Presently, all with shining faces and fresh clothes, they came filing back to the living room again.

Bunny and Robin Hood, who had changed too, were standing by the open door, their faces gleaming with—

"Why the sun's out!" Rosie cried.

"Better than that," Robin Hood said. "Come here. The rain has left you a present."

The Big Eight rushed out of doors.

"Oh-h-h-h!" they cried in unison.

A rainbow arched over the western sky. Not arched really, circled almost. For it was much rounder than the mere curve that one sees in flat country.

"I never saw such a big rainbow in my life," Laura gasped.

"If we were on the top of a very high mountain," Robin Hood explained, "we'd see the rainbow as a complete circle."

"Let's run up the—" Rosie began. "But what an idiot I am! I was going to say let's run up to the top of the mountain. But that would take us *hours* and in the meantime, where would the rainbow be?"

"Don't worry, Rosie," Bunny comforted

her. "We'll see lots of rainbows while we're here—and maybe sometime while we're climbing a mountain."

In the meantime, Silva had run upstairs, had returned with her sketch book and her black tin box of water colors. "I know what I'm going to collect for Mr. Westabrook," she cried joyfully, *"rainbows!"*

She put the paintbox on the rail, hurriedly filled the tiny china containers with paint, began to block in her composition in slashing strokes of her pencil. Then came the color. The others drew around her, watched while the rainbow slowly faded from the sky.

"This is good practise," Silva said half to them, half to herself, "working so fast. I've got to get it right the first time."

"It's nice," Robin Hood approved as her busy fingers stopped. "Very nice, indeed."

"It looks . . . sort of . . . unfinished," Silva quavered apologetically.

"It's what it pretends to be and no more," Robin Hood assured her, "a hasty sketch."

"It's amazing," he said to Bunny as they followed the children indoors, "how much movement—or perhaps I mean life—that child gets into her sketches. I could almost feel the mountain breeze blowing in that one."

Maida had fallen into concentrated, deep thought. Suddenly her seriousness broke. "I know what to call our waterfall," she exclaimed, her look all sparkles of joy, "Rainbow Waterfall."

"And let's call the brook, Bubbles Brook," Silva suggested.

CHAPTER XI

THE BIG EIGHT CALL ON NEIGHBORS

WHEN the boys started for the lake the next morning, they were loaded with fishing gear. "Mighty fishers!" Arthur, who with Robin Hood led the procession, commented as he looked back along the line.

The day seemed more than usually clear after the rain. And as the hot sun dried the trees, the shrubs and the flowers, it evoked from them all their perfume.

"What a lovely day!" the girls kept saying to each other.

They crossed the rustic bridge and walked to the lake on the farther side of the brook. They developed an excited interest in everything new, for Robin Hood was rapidly turning them into trained observers. No bird flashed across the sky that they did not watch. No new tree, bush, or flower but caught their instant attention. Also now, of course, that Laura had become a collector of leaves and Maida of flowers, all were agog to add to their treasures. After a long and rather leisurely progress, they reached the point where the brook ran into the lake.

"Let's continue along this side of the lake," Robin Hood suggested. "There's another brook which runs into it and I think we might start fishing there."

"What is the name of this lake, Robin Hood?" Tyma asked.

"Opal Lake," Robin Hood answered.

"Oh, what a beautiful name!" Silva sighed. "How I do love things that have changing colors in them—the aurora borealis, rainbows, opals, prisms and soap bubbles even. Why did they give it that name, Robin Hood?"

"The people whom I first visited named it," Robin Hood explained. "The first time they came here, they arrived at sunset. The sky was full of pink and blue clouds and the whole lake was covered with the reflection. Instantly Mrs. Delafield said, 'Why it looks like a colossal opal.' There's another lake further that they named—"

"What's that!" Arthur interrupted in a breathless voice.

Sound had burst from the direction of the lake; sound so loud and so explosive that it was almost like a cannon shot.

"I did not mean to interrupt," Arthur apologized instantly. "But what was that?" he added breathlessly.

Robin Hood was smiling. "I brought you around the lake in this direction because I hoped we'd hear that. There's a beaver dam here and I want you to see it. As we came along, I noticed that there was a beaver swimming in the lake. I didn't say anything because I wanted the thing to happen that did happen. A beaver has a broad, flat tail. When he's frightened, he dives and makes for home. But just before he sinks, he hits the water with his tail. That's his danger signal to the rest of the beavers. When they hear it, down they go."

"A beaver dam!" Arthur breathed. He threw down his fishing rod, turned a delighted, excited face to the other children. "I don't want to fish," he exclaimed. "I want to see that beaver dam. And a beaver too."

With one accord the children dropped their fishing rods beside Arthur's.

"It means keeping very still—seeing a beaver," Robin Hood warned them.

The Big Eight nodded their assent.

"All right, then," Robin Hood agreed, "we'll wait. Perhaps the beaver will come to the top of the water later. But we won't start watching just yet. I'll show you the dam first."

They proceeded along the side of the lake until they came to the brook which Robin Hood had promised them. Close to the lake shore just beyond—between them and the nearest bank of the brook—lay the dam.

Superficially it did not look like a dam at all. It looked more as though a load of branches, floating on a torrent of water, had got caught by some obstruction, and stayed wedged.

"You see," Robin Hood was explaining as they approached this structure, "the beaver can swim under water but he cannot stay there indefinitely. He requires air just as we do. So he builds these houselike structures. He builds at the top little compartments which we call 'lodges.' The beavers come up into them through the water. They are open to the air at the top. Our little friend now feels himself safe from us. He's in one of these little cubicles."

"What do they live on?" Dicky asked.

"Bark mostly. They like to build near growths of poplar—you notice there are poplar trees here. But they especially enjoy the alder—there are alders here too. Look about for a few minutes and see what you can find."

The children studied the ground carefully. Harold, to Arthur's great disgust, found the first treasure and almost immediately, Rosie, to his even greater disgust, found the second one. These were pieces of branch, a foot to a foot and a half in length, which the beavers had gnawed off, leaving an end pointed like a lead pencil.

Gradually each member of the Big Eight found a similar specimen of beaver handiwork.

"Can we take them away, Robin Hood?" Arthur asked.

"Certainly," Robin Hood answered promptly. "The beaver has no use for them and if he wants more branches, there are plenty of trees about him. Now if we want to see one, we'll have to sit here for a long time. When I say a long time, I mean a long time. It might be an hour before he appears but I think it won't be as long as that. How about it?"

All eight heads nodded violently.

"Very well," Robin Hood agreed. "Let's find a place where we have a stage box view of the proceedings and where we will be as comfortable as possible."

"I suppose we all admire beavers," Rosie said, "because we've all been taught how busy they keep. Beavers and bees and ants."

"'Go to the ant, thou sluggard!'" Robin Hood quoted. "And, 'How doth the busy little bee employ each shining hour!' I can't seem to think of any line about the beaver," he concluded regretfully. "Oh yes, 'work like a beaver.'"

"What would happen, Robin Hood," Maida asked earnestly, "if we would wade out and break up their dam?"

"We can't be a hundred per cent sure what would happen, but I think they would probably wait around for a while to see that they were not invaded again. Then they would just start in and rebuild it."

"But could they live on the land if they were forced to it?" Tyma asked.

"Undoubtedly," Robin Hood answered.

"I think it's very strange, then," Tyma continued, "that they go to all that trouble to build a dam."

"A beaver is a slow, short-legged animal," Robin Hood answered. "He would be fairly helpless against eagles, wildcats and wolves. So would prairie dogs and woodchucks—they dig holes for protection. Beavers build these houses in the water."

All the time he was studying the foreground. Not far away the land rose in a gentle swell. On it a spinney of alders shook their flashing leaves in the breeze.

"Suppose we sit there," Robin Hood suggested. "We'll all have a tree to rest our backs against."

The Big Eight rushed to the spinney. But once there, they waited for Robin Hood to tell them where to sit. Presently they were comfortably disposed in a long line, each pair to a tree.

"Now we've got to stop talking," Robin Hood said, "and we mustn't move."

Dead silence fell on the group. The Big Eight seemed to turn to statues. Occasionally an arm sank gently to a side and a leg moved with infinitesimal slowness. They waited and waited and waited. Five minutes of motionless silence is a long time for a child. Ten minutes is not twice, but four times as long. Fifteen minutes went by. Twenty minutes passed. And then—

Suddenly above the smooth water of the lake, not very far beyond the dam, a head appeared. Flat, pointed, bright-eyed, sleek, wet, glistening—it moved through the lake apparently bodiless.

And then appeared another head and another and another and . . . five!

The beavers swam for a bit. Then, two of them disappeared under the water. Three approached the shore. They darted here and there, through the grass stopping at this point and that to gnaw at an alder trunk. Then they returned to the lake. Two dove beneath the surface and disappeared. One—for what purpose, none of the Big Eight could guess—disported himself along the surface of the water. Still the Big Eight sat like statues, watching avidly. And then . . .

"Oh, here you are!" Bunny's voice sounded, and Bunny, herself, appeared on the trail.

Instantly came from the lake a report like a cannon.

Bunny, of course, was utterly unprepared for this explosion. With a little cry of fright she ran to Robin Hood, "What was that, Robin?" she asked. "I'm frightened."

Robin put his arm about her and patted her

head just as he would have done in the case of one of the Big Eight. "It's only a beaver slapping the water with his tail, Bunny," he explained. "And it's not surprising you're frightened. We were all frightened when we first heard it."

Bunny's underlip trembled a little as though she were about to cry. But in an instant she controlled her panic. "I never heard that before, but I'm glad I've heard it now," she said gallantly.

"I'm rather glad you came along, Bunny," Robin Hood said. "I wanted to hear the beaver slap the water again, but I didn't want to frighten him."

The Big Eight burst into a hubbub of explanations to Bunny, of wondering and delighted comment.

"I'm coming here, Robin Hood, early tomorrow morning," Arthur announced, "that is, if you don't mind. I'd like to watch the beaver as much as I can."

"Come every morning if you want," Robin Hood gave his permission. "I'm afraid we haven't got any time left to fish today," he went on, looking at his watch. "If we start home now, we'll get back just in time for luncheon."

The children talked of nothing but the beaver all the way back.

"I know what I'm going to do as my present

to Mr. Westabrook," Arthur exclaimed suddenly. "I'm going to keep a diary, describing all the animals I see. I'll begin with the deer that we saw the day before yesterday. I'll describe the spot where I see the animals, how they look and what they do."

"Then there's the red fox, Arthur," Rosie suggested.

"Yes, the red fox, yesterday," Arthur agreed jubilantly. "And the beaver, today. I'm going to try to see as many animals as I can. If sitting quiet will turn the trick, I'll keep as still as a post for hours. Oh boy!" Arthur burst out in what was almost an unbearable ecstasy.

On the trail ahead of the party, Arthur turned three cartwheels in swift succession.

CHAPTER XII

THE CAMP SETTLES DOWN

GRADUALLY life fell into a pattern at Camp Crescent Moon.

For a week Robin Hood kept up what might be called his forest training. Mornings after breakfast, and afternoons after luncheon, found him and Bunny, the Big Eight in tow, in the forest. Each day, Robin Hood conducted his train by a different route and, each day, deeper and deeper into its mysterious green recesses before he turned them loose to find their way back to camp. Members of the Big Eight continued to get lost for a day or two, but they were on their mettle and they improved by leaps and bounds. In the final three days of tryout, every one of them made his way homeward with a swift directness that filled Robin Hood with pride.

At the end of the week, Robin Hood pronounced them all graduates of his forestry school.

By this time, just as in the Little House at home, there had appeared on one of the walls of the living room in the chalet a bulletin board.

"Now you can, any one of you, go into the forest, at any time, alone," Robin Hood declared. "But unless I have given you special permission, I do not expect you to stay more than two hours. When you leave, you must put your name on the bulletin board and, beside it, the exact time that you left. Remember! Anybody who fails to do that will forfeit his forest privileges for three days. As I have told you, if—at the end of two hours—you have not returned, we shall have to organize a searching party."

The Big Eight took advantage of this permission with varying degrees of interest. From now on, the group explorations ceased. But the girls were likely to take their walks among the trees in pairs, trios or quartettes. No one of them seemed to have the impulse to follow the trails very far alone. The boys tended to go in pairs. Arthur, for instance, was the only one to ask permission for a solo safari. Robin Hood, however, always gave him that permission. Sometimes Arthur got up early in the morning. After his first trip, Robin Hood extended his time. And then, rising at five sometimes, Arthur would be back at eight, ready, after his early sandwich and cold milk, to sit down to a hot breakfast.

Out of Robin Hood's suitcase had come

an extremely interesting book—*Adirondack Mammals* by Dr. Hart Merriman. All the Big Eight looked through it. Some read it. But Arthur pored over it.

"If I can only see a specimen of every one of those animals, Robin Hood," he said wistfully, "I shall be—oh, boy! I'd like to make a complete category of the animals here for Mr. Westabrook."

"That reminds me, Arthur," Tyma broke in eagerly, "I thought—as long as you weren't making a map—I'd make a map of the camp for Mr. Westabrook. I don't make such good maps as you do, but Silva said she'd help me make it look like those in pirate books with sea serpents in the lake and ships with sails."

"I'll help you, too, Tyma," Arthur offered. "If there's anything you'd like me to do."

"I'll need help fast enough," Tyma agreed.

"I've decided," Harold struck in, "to make a collection for Mr. Westabrook of some of the strange things I see everywhere."

"What do you mean—'strange things'—Harold?" Robin Hood inquired.

"Well, I've come across the queerest growths at the foot of trees or even on them," Harold answered. "I don't know whether they're lichens, mushrooms or diseases. Anyway they're all very interesting and some of them—well, I'd say they were beautiful. Then sometimes I see leaves with odd scars or bruised places—very glossy. All these things interest me a lot and I think Mr. Westabrook might like to see them, too."

"I'm sure he would," Robin Hood approved heartily.

As far as individual enjoyment was concerned, Harold became more and more allured by the mountains. The mountain trails were fairly well defined. Robin Hood showed little fear that they would be lost. Harold and Tyma—between whom was developing a greater and greater congeniality—climbed the mountains again and again together. But after the mountains, they seemed most to enjoy fishing in the lake.

Arthur scaled mountains, too, but somehow their more, wide-flung, open mystery did not seem to thrill him as did the silent, secretive mystery of the woods. As for Opal Lake, again and again he accompanied the boys fishing. But sooner or later he abandoned his rod to skirt the shore to the beaver dam. There silent and motionless as a wooden image, he watched the doings of its active little inhabitants.

In that hour or two of lamplight at night, before the whole household went to bed, the Big Eight were a busy group.

Rosie was working hard knitting a pair of socks for Mr. Westabrook. At first, "I never am going to learn how to knit, Bunny," she declared hopelessly again and again. "I hate to have you try to teach me because you're going to realize what an idiot I am. I'm about the stupidest girl that ever lived."

"You're not stupid at all," Bunny would reassure her, "and you're learning faster than I did. Turning a heel is what my mother called a 'footy' job. Now we'll make a fresh start. One day it will all come to you, Rosie."

Suddenly—apparently—it did all come to Rosie. "I believe I've got the hang of it, Bunny," she cried enthusiastically one night. "Gee, isn't this fun!"

Now the clatter of Rosie's needles added its tiny domestic note to the quiet of the evening work.

"Bunny," Maida exclaimed once, "just as soon as I've finished my collection, I want you to teach me to knit. I think its perfectly fascinating to see those socks grow."

"And the sound is so pretty," Silva observed.

"I like the sound too," Dicky exclaimed.

"Don't tell me you're going to write a knitting symphony," Rosie joked him.

"I hadn't thought of that," Dicky smiled. "But now that you suggest it, perhaps I will."

At these evening sessions, Maida and Laura sat at the ample central table with the big blankbooks, and paste pots, steadily pressing leaves and flowers. Now and then, they stopped to ask Bunny's advice. But for the most part they worked in a concentration that seemed to leave them speechless.

Across the table from them sat Tyma with the big sheet of white paper on which he was making his map. Starting it in pencil, of course, he seemed to spend the first two or three evenings mainly sketching and rubbing out. He got up again and again to study the huge map of the county which hung on the wall of the living room, came back and made corrections.

"Want any help?" Arthur asked occasionally, working at his reports a little distance around the table from Tyma.

"Yes!" Tyma growled, "nothing but. I wish you'd do the whole doggone map for me. But I don't want you to look at it until I've something there for you to look at."

"All right," Arthur answered cheerfully, "tell me when you're ready."

Arthur immediately lost himself in his own writing and drawing. For Arthur was producing what might really be called a work. It was a diary. He had already entered in it under the date of their first breakfast, an account of the deer feeding by the brook. On the next page, he made a sketch of the browsing animals. Arthur was not a natural artist like Silva but he kept stubbornly at it. With the help of illustrations from various books, he finally finished his picture.

"They look like stuffed deer," he sighed despondently. "But I guess they'll have to do."

"I think it's very nice," Bunny encouraged him.

Under the proper date the red fox had gone into the work and under several dates, all Arthur's observations in regard to the beaver. But he had sought and found adventures in the forest and these he discussed with the excited Big Eight. Twice, he had seen woodchuck; any number of times, little green snakes. But these, although he had recorded them faithfully, had not excited him unduly; for woodchuck and harmless green snakes were not uncommon in the vicinity of the Little House. Once in the forest, however, resting quietly in the crotch of a tree, sound and movement below had attracted him. A lovely doe, followed by her no less lovely fawn, had strolled into sight, were nibbling the ground with that delicate precision which, he had learned, marked these animals. He watched them, noting particularly the patternlike spotting of the baby's pelt, until, still feeding, they had disappeared into a tangled green tunnel of trees. Last of all, on the further side of the lake he had caught sight—a mere flashing glimpse—of a creature that he was sure was an otter. And then—best luck of all—he had come upon a raccoon.

"I knew him by the rings on his tail," he asserted, busily making a sketch. "Oh, gee," he concluded finally, "I wanted to call this picture *Raccoon Walking* but it looks just as though he was lying down."

Maida tiptoed over and looked over his shoulder. "So it does," she agreed. "Why not call it *Raccoon Lying Down?*"

"Why not?" Arthur agreed. "Maida, that's a magnificent suggestion. Girls are very useful sometimes."

Maida smiled. "Singularly enough, Arthur," she replied with spirit, "—and I know you're not going to believe this—I have sometimes found that true of boys."

"Smarty," Arthur scoffed. "If I can see a possum," Arthur reverted to his longings, "or—oh, gee—if I could only see a wildcat. And would I be happy if I could run across a bear. Boy, you don't, any of you, know the half of it."

After every expedition into the forest, someone would say, "Did you see a wildcat, Arthur?" or, "Did you run into a bear?" Bunny even remembered another animal whom Arthur might have encountered, "How about Cousin Lynx?"

Dolefully always, Arthur shook his head, "Not yet!" he would answer.

Harold's collection was growing amain. Mrs. Dore had taken the books from one of the long shelves of the glassed-in bookcase, so that he could use it to hold his specimens. Strange forest treasure of various kinds—the children examined them all minutely while Robin Hood discoursed learnedly on them.

"I think, Harold, you're making the most interesting collection of all," Rosie said once, "because they're all things that you can take up in your hands and look at through a microscope."

Sometimes from the piano came strange sounds as Dicky tried to arrange combinations of notes that simulated falling water. As always, Maida encouraged him constantly, "I like that very much, Dicky. It's very tinkling and soft. No, I don't like that so much. Try the other again. Why don't you put those notes down? That's the best you've done yet."

"If I could only get one page," Dicky sighed, "not regular music. Of course I can't compose regular music. But just a collection of notes that sounded the way falling water does."

"They would delight father," Maida assured him. "It would be like a bouquet, but not of flowers, a bouquet of sounds."

CHAPTER XIII

THE CAMP SETTLES DOWN STILL FURTHER

BUT Arthur was not the only one of the Big Eight who performed his explorations solitary and alone.

Maida, for instance, was likely to take a book out under one of the big trees within sight of the camp, and read for an hour or two. All kinds of things happened to her there and she welcomed such charming interruptions. Squirrels ran back and forth, up and down trees, sometimes scolded her violently from a safe bough. Once, one of them dropped a shell of a nut close beside her. Whether this was a sign of approval or disapproval Maida of course did not know. But she kept so quiet that finally the squirrels became used to her presence and approached amazingly close. That gave her an idea and the next time she came to her favorite seat, she brought some nuts with her, scattered them a little distance off. After a while, the squirrels came for them, took them one by one away. She put nuts nearer and nearer. And gradually, the bright-eyed little creatures came closer and closer. However, she never could get them to feed from her hand, as squirrels on Boston Common had often done.

Whenever a rainbow appeared, Silva would rush dashing into the house for her paints, come dashing out again. Her picture was naturally hurried, often a little uncertain in touch, and tremulous in color. But she was scrupulous about not retouching this first sketch. After the rainbow had disappeared, however, she made a second sketch, putting in the surroundings with a more careful detail. This meant, of course, two pictures to every rainbow. Already, she had a collection of eight.

Maida always sat near Silva as she worked. "Oh, I think it's beautiful, Silva," she would say.

"But the drawing is very bad," Silva always answered with a combination of exasperation and resignation. "Of course, I don't draw as well as I should and the hurry with which I have to work makes it even worse."

"But you said, yourself," Maida pointed out, "that this was the best practice in the world."

"It is," Silva reiterated. "And I'm so glad to have it."

"I know just what you mean by the drawing not being good," Maida added honestly. "Of course, it isn't as good as it will be, but you're improving all the time. You get better and better. I can see that. But there's something about the colors you choose, Silva. Everything you do seems alive to me."

"I'm so glad you feel that way," Silva said humbly, "for sometimes I feel very discouraged."

Rosie herself said that when she made a vow to collect trees, she had no idea what she really meant. But now, she was collecting them by climbing them. Her experiments entertained Bunny and Robin Hood inordinately.

One after another Rosie had ascended all the climbable trees at the edge of the camp. Bunny and Mrs. Dore and Robin Hood would perhaps be enjoying their customary afternoon tea on the piazza of the chalet when a voice, apparently coming from the clouds, would call, "Look where I am! Look where I am!"

Somewhere in a big tree, her beret separating the green leaves with its scarlet flame, would appear Rosie's sparkling face, her slim, lithe figure.

"Oh, she's so high up," Mrs. Dore always commented. "You don't think she'll fall, Mr. Hood?"

"I feel very certain she won't," Robin Hood would answer. "I've watched her again and again. She seems daring, but it's only because instinctively she knows just where to put her feet and hands. Rosie climbs just like a cat. She feels each branch out before she puts her feet on it. But she's got so much instinct that it's almost as though she were running up a flight of stairs."

This sometimes set up a rivalry in the boys. They would even go up the tree after Rosie, or try to get higher up on a neighboring one. But although they were, like most boys, good tree climbers, the sight of a tall monarch of the forest did not seem to arouse in their breasts what immediately it aroused in Rosie's—the desire for conquest.

Robin Hood was observing all these changes with the utmost interest, care and minuteness. He talked them over for long periods with Bunny. Of Silva alone they had no doubt so far as definite gifts were concerned. Silva would, undoubtedly, choose a career—if not that of an artist—something that was connected with artistic expression. With Laura, he felt more and more that dancing was a major passion; all other interests seemed minor. As to Rosie, he could prophesy nothing—except that she would have efficiency, accuracy, speed. Rosie could fill any executive position, he thought, that required these qualities plus sympathy with people and enjoyment of them. Of Maida, he was most uncertain. But the fact that Maida would inherit a great fortune and that, in consequence, it was not necessary for her to earn her living might easily enough delay development.

When it came to the boys, Arthur interested Robin Hood most. Arthur had a profound interest in all things of the out-of-doors. He was so concentrated that he could work for hours, not noting the passing of time. He had physical strength, physical courage and a great moral integrity. Arthur would go far. By this time, however, Robin Hood knew that Arthur, himself, must decide what Arthur would be.

Tyma—well, Tyma had said he wanted to be a sailor and until something happened to prove the contrary, Robin Hood decided that he would look at Tyma entirely from that point of view. Tyma had great physical strength and endurance. It looked as though Tyma had made a correct diagnosis of his own ambition.

Harold again was something of an enigma. Harold had said that he loved mountains and would like to climb them. His experience in camp was proving this to be true. But mountain-climbing could not be a vocation. With most people it must be an avocation. Harold had, more than any other child in the group, the power to command and to see that his commands were carried out. Robin Hood often felt that in a tight corner he would most prefer, next to Arthur, to have Harold beside him.

Curiously enough Harold could obey command as swiftly and efficiently as he could give it.

Dicky was absorbed in music just as Silva was absorbed in painting. Robin Hood decided that they would perhaps have to wait longer for those two to develop than any of the others of the Big Eight. Experience had taught him that many children start with ambitions in the arts—to write books, to paint pictures, to make statuary, to compose music, to act. But as they grow towards manhood and womanhood, they often find that they have failed to develop the necessary ability. Sometimes a second ability manifests itself. In the case of these two, Robin Hood told himself again and again, "I must keep on watch for that supplementary gift." As yet it had appeared in the case of neither.

It was a happy camp. Now that the Big Eight were freed from chaperonage, there were long periods when there was nobody in the chalet but the grown-ups.

Mrs. Dore busied herself about the house. Occasionally she walked to the brook or to the edge of the forest. But mainly she was content to occupy her leisure moments on the piazza, sewing. Regularly, three times a week after dinner, she called Granny Flynn on the telephone—always returned to the group laughing over some special expression of her mother's.

Robin Hood and Bunny explored the countryside together, coming back with treasure that they, in their turn, had picked up. But by the magic of his continual vigilance, Robin Hood always knew where every member of the Big Eight was. He began to consult his watch the instant it seemed that their absence had been prolonged. But the Big Eight gave him little trouble in this respect. Their stomachs warned them—if the watches on their wrists had not proved it to them—when the time for luncheon and dinner was approaching. And sometimes, they came home early, so that the delighted Florabelle could cook the strings of fish they brought from Opal Lake.

CHAPTER XIV

ROSIE TAKES A WALK

SINGING to herself, Rosie came into the living room to consult the bulletin board. The night before she had finished the socks which she was knitting for Mr. Westabrook and this morning, she felt rather at a loose end. Especially did she feel so when the board informed her that all the rest of the Big Eight were busy outside the chalet. She studied the entries, one after another.

The first, signed Maida and Laura, read: "Have gone to Opal Lake to get some leaves and flowers that we saw there yesterday." Silva had written: "Am at Rainbow Waterfall completing the sketch I made the other day." Tyma and Harold were at their favorite occupation—fishing; Arthur, at one of his favorite occupations—watching the beaver. Rosie did not have to ask where Dicky was. Back to her, pencil in hand, he sat at the piano, before him a sheet of music such as musicians use in composition, industriously thumping out notes and occasionally registering one on the paper. He was completely unconscious of Rosie's presence and Rosie stole out without a word to him.

What to do, she wondered, or where to go?

It was a beautiful morning, clear as a crystal, but with a little tang of cold at its heart. Rosie wore her slacks and her scarlet beret. But as she passed the row of hooks near the door, that tiny tingle of cold in the air moved her to don her scarlet cape. Leisurely she surveyed the landscape. In the distance, she could see Silva, squatted on her little stool, apparently painting busily. She would not join Silva, Rosie thought, because she would only disturb her. She would not join Maida and Laura because she would only disturb them. If she approached Arthur, he would scowl blackly at her for sending the beavers scuttling into their lodges. She would not join Tyma and Harold. Rosie had discovered that she did not enjoy fishing. Sometimes she cried when a dying fish flopped about her feet.

Suddenly an idea struck her. This was the predestined time for her to make her first expedition alone into the forest.

She glided back noiselessly into the living room. First consulting her wrist watch, she wrote on the board, "nine-thirty. Starting to explore the impenetrable forest. If not back by eleven-thirty, send rescue party." Putting her hand to her throat, she made sure the policeman's whistle hung about her neck. Examining the pocket in her blouse, she saw that the compass was there. Then she stole out of the house.

As she took up the trail into the forest, Rosie could hear Bunny's voice from the side piazza. Bunny was reading aloud to Robin Hood a new chapter in the book she was writing. As she passed the ell, she could hear Florabelle's cheerful accents warning Zeke to look out for snakes. Rosie pursued the trail to its entrance into the forest in a leisurely manner, stopping to pick a flower here, to watch a bird's flight there. Presently, in a crevice of a rock, an acorn of unusual size attracted her. Last year's crop, but still sound. Immediately the thought of Betsy Hale flashed into her mind—Betsy with her dolls' table set with a quaint mixture of tiny dishes in china and tin with acorn cups beside them. She would take this acorn home to Betsy, she decided. Perhaps she could collect enough to make a dinner set. She put it into the pocket of her slacks.

There, her hand encountered a thick wad of folded paper. Pulling it out into the light, she discovered it was a sheet of bright scarlet tissue, which—its color attracting her as scarlet always did—she had salvaged from a package which had come to the Little House. Looking at it for an instant, an idea suddenly flashed into her mind. Obviously that idea amused her, for her bright lips parted in a mischievous smile.

Carefully she tore the paper into tiny pieces, stuffed her right-hand pocket with them. Then, her mind filled with fairy tales that she had read, she dropped a piece of the red paper at intervals along the way.

"It's like a trail of blood," she thought, still smiling.

Maida had told Rosie that she was always conscious of a kind of terror when she walked in the woods. It was a pleasant terror, she admitted, but still a terror. She said that always she had the feeling that the trees were closing in stealthily around her—almost as though they were great, grave, green creatures of the forest who were conspiring to make a prisoner of her. And then, Maida added, the strange hush, the cathedrallike silence—at those moments when neither bird nor insect made a sound—filled her with a kind of awe.

"The queer thing about it is, Rosie," Maida concluded, "I'm not afraid of live creatures. It would not occur to me that there would be bears or wildcats or lynxes about. But I have a feeling that if I could only see far enough and clearly enough—and if I were only quick enough—I'd catch a dryad or a satyr talking together, or I'd come across a group of fairies dancing in a ring. I'm always looking for something that I never see."

Rosie thought of that now, but mainly to note that she had no such sensation. It was true that the trees seemed to march in around her as though to veil the path but she felt that she was the mistress of the situation—not the trees. Sudden sounds and movements did not bother her—the grey squirrel who suddenly, on her advance, shot up a tree like a shaft of grey lightning and, from a safe height, paused to scold her violently; the birds who, as she appeared, suddenly broke out into an uproar of indignation and who, as she passed, suddenly lapsed into the silence of complete forgiveness.

No, independent, as far as nerves were concerned, of all these interruptions, Rosie pursued her way, studying this tree and that, this rock and that; noting moss, lichens, flowers, leaves, parasitical growths; garnering questions about them. And mechanically now, her hand went to her pocket, withdrew a fragment or two of red paper, dropped it along the way.

"It's like confetti," Rosie said, "just as though I were a bride in a scarlet wedding."

It amused her to think of a scarlet wedding and she drew an imaginary picture of the bride with a long veil of scarlet tulle and the church filled with scarlet poppies, scarlet candles.

Under the impetus of these amusing thoughts Rosie's pace quickened. She was still careful, however, to note landmarks or trailmarks as the Big Eight called them now.

Presently she realized that she had gone deeper into the forest than ever before. The thought thrilled her. She looked at her watch. She had been gone three quarters of an hour. Fifteen minutes more and it would be time for her to start back.

Suddenly she caught the sound of running water. She paused, listened. There must be a rivulet just ahead. After a while, she came to a little glade where flowed a tiny stream. It was a charming spot—mossy by the water and bright here and there with flowers. Beyond and just ahead, bushes bunched thickly on both sides of the trail and then the great trees shot up again. Rosie knelt at the brookside, scooped up palmfuls of the delicious water, drank deeply. Leaping again on to her feet, she found that she was standing at the foot of a magnificent oak with low-growing branches.

"What a beauty!" she thought. And then, "And how safe! If this oak only grew by the Little House, we could gradually teach all the Little Seven to climb trees."

Tree-climbing, of course, was, in Rosie's estimation, a valuable accomplishment.

She was to prove that to be true in a brief interval. But for another moment she stood enjoying the coolness and greenness of the pretty glade.

And then suddenly the crash of snapping

branches startled her. Something was breaking through the bush on the other side of the stream—a something that came nearer and nearer—a something big that was obviously parting the braided boughs with a powerful head . . .

All kinds of ideas flashed through Rosie's mind. Could it be a stray horse? Or a cow? Perhaps it was deer? Maybe a wildcat. At this thought her heart contracted. She reassured herself with Robin Hood's statement that wildcats never attack humans. Was it a Canadian lynx? Robin Hood hadn't said whether they attacked men or not.

And then . . .

Separated by a half a dozen rods, Rosie found herself confronting a big black bear.

Rosie turned and leaped into the arms of the convenient oak tree. She had climbed trees swiftly before, often in a race with the boys—she always won—but she had never ascended any tree as quickly as this one.

All the time she was thinking, "Bears climb trees too." But every time this thought came to her, she blanked it with another: "I'm lighter than the bear is. He can't go so high as I can. I'll sit on the very top if I have to."

She had not had time to throw off her cape, but she pushed it over her shoulders so that it hung straight down her back. After a while, she reached a crotch in the branches, so high that she believed herself to be safe. She stopped and peered downwards.

To her great delight, the bear did not seem at all angry at her presence—not even disturbed. To be sure, he started forward for a lumbering second. He stopped at her tree too—her heart turned to ice—arose on his hind legs. But that movement turned out to be merely a preliminary to a curious performance. Standing with his back against the tree, he turned his head over his shoulder and reaching as high as he could, he gnawed off a piece of bark. Having performed that satisfying operation, he lumbered down to the brook, drank long and deeply. Then he stretched himself out on a patch of sunny moss and proceeded to take a good rest.

Rosie's fears had abated. "Gee," she said to herself, "I guess this is what you call being treed. I wonder if I should begin to blow the whistle." She looked at her watch. "No, fifteen minutes yet. The bear may go off somewhere. Why don't you, little bear," she thought, trying to put a light aspect on the situation. "Way off—miles away—are plenty of good things to eat. Way off where you came from." Then the lightness disappeared from her thoughts. "I wonder, if I whistle, if that will draw his attention and he'll come up this tree after me. But I'll have to begin whistling after a while, for Robin Hood will start out to find me. Oh, dear, what shall I do. Robin Hood won't have a gun. I can't let him get too close to the bear. He can climb a tree too, of course, but maybe he won't find such a good one as this. Oh, dear! Oh, dear! Oh, dear!"

CHAPTER XV

ARTHUR TAKES A WALK

IN THE meantime, Arthur having made more than an hour's observation of the beavers, came strolling back to the camp. He went into the living room to consult the bulletin board. Dicky was still thumping away at the piano. He did not even notice that Arthur entered the room. Arthur's eyes ran down the list of entries on the bulletin board until they came to the last one written in Rosie's slanting handwriting. As though it suggested an idea to him, he wrote under it: "ten o'clock. Have loaded up with pemmican and supplies of all sorts and am going into the forest in search of Rosie. Arthur." He strolled out of the room, the absorbed Dicky still not noting his presence, and made a leisurely way back of the house to the trail. He had scarcely proceeded a dozen rods before his quick eye noted a scarlet fleck in the grass. He examined it—a tiny fragment of tissue paper.

"How did that get there?" he asked aloud.

He moved on along the beginning of the trail, now almost as familiar to him as any of those about the Little House. Another fragment of scarlet . . . another . . . and another . . . Where on earth did they come from and what on earth did they mean?

Suddenly the answer came to him. He knew that Rosie was in the forest somewhere. Scarlet! Scarlet always suggested Rosie. Undoubtedly, she had had the humorous idea of making an easy trail for herself by means of these colorful pointers. Arthur followed them but he remembered—this lesson having by this time been burned into him—to note trailmarks. Presently the little red dots took him off the main path into a new and unexplored area.

Rosie is a great girl, Arthur thought approvingly, to blaze new trails for herself. But then he had always known that Rosie was a great girl. In numberless excursions together in the old Charlestown days—when they had played hooky from school in order to explore Boston—he had found her brave, resourceful, accurate, dependable. It was a new experience for Arthur to be analyzing girls, but for the moment he found himself thinking of the girls of the Big Eight in the terms of character.

Arthur neither liked nor disliked girls. As a rule, he did not think of them at all. To him, a girl became a friend in exact proportion to her ability to conform to a boy's standards. In other words, at present, to Arthur, a girl was only a lesser boy. But girls, as a sex, he began to realize dimly now, had qualities that boys did not possess. It might be—and this was an amazing departure for Arthur—that those feminine qualities were as good as masculine qualities.

Take Maida for instance. Maida was the most truthful person Arthur had ever known. Almost never did she make the careless statements that all the rest of the Big Eight did. Perhaps, in part, she inherited this instinct for accuracy and her love of truth from her father; perhaps, in part, her training had developed it. That accuracy went beyond mere factual correctness—Arthur realized vaguely —it ran into the realm of a truth higher even than honesty. And then, in addition, Maida was not only the politest girl that Arthur had ever met, she was the kindest. Perhaps, Arthur found himself thinking, politeness came out of kindness. But then he had seen people who were polite enough who, yet, he did not like. Politeness could be only a form. But when real kindness lay back of it—oh, then it was a different thing. He guessed that Maida was a great girl too.

Silva! Perhaps, Arthur thought, he knew Silva less than any of the four girls. And that was not alone because he had known her only a year, while he had known Rosie and Laura all his life. Silva was, he rather guessed, different from other girls. And here again that difference did not arise entirely from her being a gypsy. For he knew Tyma, who was also a gypsy of course, just as well as he knew Harold. And, indeed, he understood Tyma better than he did Dicky. There was a great congeniality between him and Tyma. He guessed that there was a—a—what should he call it? A kind of mystery . . . Was that it? Yes, that was it. There was a kind of mystery of character about Silva. Not that Silva wasn't a straight-shooter. But there were all sorts of things in her by which she might grow and develop into something quite different from what she was now. It was too deep a problem in psychology for a boy. Arthur gave it up. All he knew was that he liked Silva and admired her. Yes, Silva was a great girl, too.

When it came to Laura—well, he guessed if he were making a list of the four girls according to his liking, Rosie would come first and Laura last. Often Laura irritated him. He discovered now as he searched his soul, he admired her too. For Maida had been, as Arthur would put it, born a good child. Rosie had been born a sport. Silva had been born self-contained and self-sustaining. But Laura must have been born—or perhaps she was bred—fundamentally disagreeable. When he first knew her, she was stubborn, conceited, self-assertive, selfish. But now, she was none of those things and Arthur knew, for vaguely he had felt the processes going on, that Laura had cured herself of all these unpleasant qualities. She would never develop all the sportsmanlike traits that Rosie owned. She would never surge with the warm kindness that actuated Maida. She would never possess the power of withdrawing into herself that Silva had. But she had become a great appreciator of others. This made her, in a kind of swing to the other extreme, a depreciator of herself. Too much so, Arthur thought now. By George, she ought not to be that way. He thought with a sudden wave of cordial feeling toward Laura that he was going to try to pay her some compliments. Suddenly he discovered he liked Laura too. Yes, Laura was a great girl also. "Why it's exactly as though I had four sisters," he thought suddenly.

And then to his intense surprise, he found that his eyes were wet.

On and on Arthur went swiftly. And all along the way appeared the little scarlet direction arrows that Rosie had dropped.

Suddenly in the distance, his eye caught on one of the most amazing sights it had ever seen. An enormous scarlet bird at the top of a tree. What could it be? If an eagle or a condor or a vulture had turned blood-red, that is how it would look. In another second, he realized that it was Rosie.

Instantly—she must have seen him just as he saw her—Rosie's shrill whistle rang out.

"Get up a tree as quick as you can, Arthur," Rosie screamed. "There's a bear here near the brook."

Arthur did not pause to question Rosie's command. Just off the path was a big elm growing beside a great boulder. He leaped onto the rock, jumped from the rock to a lower branch, tore up the elm as fast as he could go.

"Good boy, Arthur!" Rosie cheered him on. "You did that in a minute flat."

Arthur had gone as high as he could get. The same thoughts that had flashed through Rosie's mind, flashed through his. Would the bear climb the tree after him? The bear was heavier than he was; he could not possibly get so high.

And then he caught sight of the creature. Evidently Rosie's whistle and her cry had disturbed him. He came at a swift lumber down the path towards Arthur's elm. Arthur watched his approach in a kind of panic. Would bruin leap onto the rock and clamber up the tree? But even then, a spot in a part of his brain, coolly remote from terror, was registering notes for his list of animals—black in color—pretty big—how curiously he runs, placing each front paw, one far ahead of the other, turning his head from one side to the other with each forward step—why he runs like a swimmer doing the trudgeon stroke—he doesn't seem to be coming fast, but boy, can he go! . . .

The bear did not pause. He ran on down the trail for a moment, then turned off at the left. Arthur could hear him crashing through bushes for a while. Then the sounds died into silence.

"Gosh, Rosie," Arthur called, "where did you scare up that bear?"

"I was standing by the brook here," Rosie called back in answer, "when he suddenly came tearing through the bushes. I went up this oak like a monkey. I never climbed so fast in my life, Arthur. I'd have taken all prizes in any tree-climbing contest."

"I bet I beat you," Arthur boasted.

"I bet you didn't. And now what shall we do?"

"We'd better wait a while," Arthur counselled. "I believe there's no danger of that bear's coming back. I think I've read that when they are disturbed, they beat it off as far as they can get. We'll wait fifteen minutes. I want to save Robin Hood from coming after us."

They waited the quarter of an hour. Then they scrambled down the trees and started homewards. No strolling now. No stopping to look at natural features. No watching for trailmarks. They followed Rosie's scarlet confetti and they made such time as they would not have dreamed was possible. When they burst into the chalet, everybody had gathered for luncheon.

"We saw a bear!" Rosie panted, sinking into a chair.

"A great big black one!" Arthur added, sinking into a chair, too.

"I saw him first," Rosie added. "And got into a tree. When I saw Arthur coming, I whistled and called to him. That frightened the bear off."

"Then we were treed for about twenty minutes," Arthur took it up.

"A bear!" Robin Hood repeated. He smiled, but his eyes were serious. "He's probably miles away from here now. But I think that means that I'm going to forbid any walks in the forest for a while."

CHAPTER XVI

THE CAMP ENTERTAINS A NOCTURNAL VISITOR

OF COURSE they talked about the bear all day long. Not one of the Big Eight left the piazza, except to stroll away a few rods. But from time to time the boys cast wistful looks in the direction of the forest.

Robin Hood intercepted one of these longing glances. "I know what you boys want," he said. "You'd like me to give you each a gun, so that we could all hunt the bear. That's perfectly natural, but I'd like to ask you one thing. Would you really like to kill him?"

The four boys shook their heads violently.

"That's it," Robin Hood pointed out. "You'd like to see him, but you wouldn't want to hurt him. However, I think you are a little too young to hunt bears. Besides, by this time, he's probably in the next county."

Bunny decided that this was a good time to teach the other three girls to knit. And so, she provided them all with needles and worsted, with Rosie's assistance started instruction. Laura, as might be expected, developed almost instantly into an expert. But as Maida said, it was a race between her and Silva as to which could make the most mistakes. But they refused to be discouraged because they had watched Mr. Westabrook's socks grow so steadily under Rosie's newly skillful fingers and because the process really fascinated them.

The boys watched this feminine work for a while. Then Arthur said, "If I stay here another moment, I'll be learning to knit, myself."

"I can knit," Robin Hood informed them. "Plenty of men do, in illness or loneliness."

"Then, if you knit, Robin Hood," Arthur declared, "I'm going to learn sometime. I'm too excited today though."

"Let's put out the croquet set," Robin Hood suggested. "Then after you've had a little practice we might organize a tournament."

"I didn't know there was a croquet set here," Harold exclaimed in a delighted voice. "Gee, I love croquet."

"I've never played the game," Arthur admitted. "But I'm sure I'll like it—today anyway. I'd like any game today."

"You'll like it all right," Harold prophesied.

The croquet box was on a top shelf in the big gun closet in the hall. The boys brought it out. Then, with lawn mower, rakes and hoes, they cleaned off a level area in front of the chalet. Then, using a long flexible measuring tape, they set off distances in careful accordance with the instructions pasted on the inside of the cover of the croquet box. This engaged them for several hours, for Robin Hood was meticulous in regard to stones or dead twigs or protruding roots. The shadows were beginning to lengthen when the wickets were in place. Then the girls dropped their knitting and Robin Hood matched them in partnerships. Harold, who he knew would be the best player, with Silva, who he suspected would be the worst; Arthur with Maida; Dicky with Laura; Tyma with Rosie.

Never had the Big Eight laughed harder, for although Harold made some skillful shots—one of them the entire length of the field—the others outdid each other in awkwardness. But they were all fascinated by the sport. When they dropped their mallets to swarm around the tea table on the piazza, "I certainly am going to practice up on that game," Arthur declared. "I ought to play with wickets as wide as barrel hoops."

The grown-ups were drinking tea with toast and honey. The children drank ginger ale. "But no honey for you now," Mrs. Dore ruled. "I'm afraid it will spoil your appetite for dinner. But you may each have two cookies."

The Big Eight looked longingly at the great open-mouthed jar of honey. But they soon forgot their disappointment when they swarmed back to the croquet ground.

Florabelle and Zeke came out to clear the tea things away.

"Florabelle," Robin Hood addressed her, "and Zeke, I want to tell you that Rosie and Arthur saw a bear in the forest today. They frightened him away and he's probably many miles from here now. I just tell you so that when you are out-of-doors, you can keep your eyes open."

"I ain't afraid of no *bear,*" Florabelle declared with contemptuous emphasis. "I ain't afraid of nothing up here," she asserted with vigor. "I *is* afraid of snakes though," she added.

"Well, this boy is afraid of bear," Zeke admitted with equal certainty. "Yes, *sir!* Old man bear better keep away from my door."

Nevertheless, despite her scorn of bruin, Florabelle went into the house forgetting to bring the big open-mouthed jar of honey back with her.

Never was talk among the Big Eight more animated than that night at dinner. Rosie was excited because she had seen the bear. And Arthur was equally jubilant. He had not only seen a bear, but he could make it the climax to his descriptions of animals for Mr. Westabrook. Both Maida and Laura had, that day, added handsomely to their collections. And they were all amused and interested by the prospect of a croquet tournament. They asked Robin Hood many questions about the procedure of a tournament.

After dinner, as usual, they gathered about the big round table in the living room. The big student lamp in the center cast a pleasant, even glow, which made minute work easy. They never pulled curtains over the long glass windows. For first of all there were no curtains to pull and then they liked to bring the night into the room. The windows came to the very floor. Occasionally one of the Big Eight would stroll to the window and, shielding his eyes from the lamplight with his hands, would look out into the deep blue distance, where stars lay like silver powder.

There had come an interval of almost complete silence, for everybody was busy. Mrs. Dore and Bunny had gone upstairs on some housekeeping errand. Robin Hood sat at one side of the fireplace, Harold and Dicky near him reading. Silva was knitting slowly and awkwardly but with an intense concentration. Maida and Laura were pasting specimens into their books. Rosie was writing a letter. Arthur was composing the first draft of his description of the bear. Tyma was working on his map. All sat at the center table.

Suddenly Arthur lifted his head. "What's that?" he exclaimed in a low, tense voice.

Robin Hood was facing the long windows

which opened on the front piazza. An instant —but only an instant later, his head came up too.

"Get up children," he called in low tones, "and go upstairs as quietly and quickly as you can. There's a bear on the front piazza. Don't get excited. You're perfectly safe. Open the door for them, Arthur."

To the eternal credit of the Big Eight they carried out Robin Hood's orders perfectly. They dropped their work quietly and arose as noiselessly as possible, softly pushing chairs out of their way.

Arthur moved slowly to the door leading to the hall, opened it, stood while the others went through.

"He's found the honey," Robin Hood reassured them softly. "Don't be frightened, children. Take your time. He won't come in here as long as there's any honey left."

All the rest of the Big Eight were out of the room now. Robin Hood motioned Arthur through the door. "Get Zeke and Florabelle upstairs, Arthur," he ordered.

Then slowly Robin Hood walked over to the table, blew out the light and followed the Big Eight. As he closed and locked the door back of him, they heard the window glass crash as the bear broke the long French windows apart and came into the living room.

While Arthur herded the rest of the Big

Eight into the back hall, a Zeke excited but apparently not frightened, and a Florabelle, highly terrified, despite all her boast to the contrary, appeared. Robin Hood busied himself in the gun closet.

"Come here, Tyma and you, Harold," he called. The rest, following his orders, had rushed upstairs—all except Arthur and Dicky who lingered, waiting for other directions.

"There are three guns here," Robin Hood said briskly. "I'll take one. You two are accustomed to shooting. I'll give this gun to you, Tyma and this to you, Harold." He gave them both a quick sharp look, "Remember what I've told you. Don't throw the safety catch off until you're ready to shoot."

Tyma and Harold nodded.

"There isn't one chance in a thousand we'll have to shoot," Robin Hood declared. "There is no earthly way the bear can get to us. But it's just as well to be armed. Now up all of you."

Upstairs they found the rest of the household gathered in the boys' room. Everybody was excited, but nobody—not even Florabelle now—was scared. Instinctively, though, they talked in low tones.

"Robin Hood," Rosie asked, "will the bear break through the door to the living room and come up here?"

"Not a chance in the world," Robin Hood reassured her.

"I'm getting to be quite fond of this bear," Rosie went on. "He must be the one Arthur and I saw today. I consider that he belongs to me."

"I suppose he's hungry," Arthur suggested.

"He found the honey on the porch," Robin Hood explained, "and there's nothing bears like more than honey."

No sound had come from below. Suddenly there was a crash.

"He's just turned a chair over," Robin Hood explained cheerfully.

"Will he stay there all night, Robin Hood?" Mrs. Dore asked.

"He may," Robin Hood answered promptly, "but I think probably not."

"If it occurs to him to curl up beside the fire," Bunny suggested, "there's no knowing when he'll wake up."

"There is that possibility," Robin Hood admitted. "But we have the advantage of him remember. We have an entrance to the base of supplies—the kitchen—and he hasn't. So this is a very unequal siege."

Sounds continued to come from below—no further crashes; only the jarring of chairs on the floor as bruin pushed them out of his path.

"I'm going to sit by the front window," Robin Hood said, "if Mr. Bear leaves the house I want to see him go. Now there's no reason why the rest of you shouldn't all go to bed. You're perfectly safe. In the first place, the bear can't get up here. In the second place, if he could, we have three guns. And in the third place, after he's explored the living room he'll probably wander off into the forest."

Everybody protested that he could not go to bed because he could not possibly sleep. They all sat around in a circle talking in low tones, occasionally stopping to listen.

Suddenly there came from downstairs a metallic clatter.

"What's he got into now?" Maida asked.

"I think he knocked the shovel and tongs down," Mrs. Dore suggested.

A long silence followed this clatter. "I believe you're right, Bunny," Mrs. Dore said thoughtfully, "I believe the bear's gone to sleep in front of the fire."

"Just like a fairy tale," Maida commented.

They sat up for an hour longer. Gradually as the silence downstairs remained unbroken, the excitement of the besieged campers died down. Zeke and Florabelle were the first to leave.

"Sleep until you wake up," Robin Hood suggested. "If by seven o'clock in the morning, the bear hasn't gone, I'll appeal to the State Police."

Next Mrs. Dore melted away with a, "I cannot keep my eyes open an instant longer."

Then, one by one, the girls disappeared, Bunny accompanying Rosie who was the last girl to leave. At first, Dicky refused to consider going to bed. But after he had fallen asleep twice, he gave in, undressed and crept in under the bed clothes. Tyma and Harold, still excited because they were manning the guns, lasted till midnight. Then, at Robin Hood's recommendation, they too crawled between the cool sheets. It was an hour later before Arthur, after repeated noddings, gave up the struggle with sleep.

Robin Hood continued to sit at the window, his gun across his knees.

It was a beautiful night. A full moon had conquered the darkness; a silvery twilight lay over the scene. Robin Hood was not alarmed by the situation. He felt that at any moment the bear might wake up and shamble off. He felt too that he had only to go downstairs, open the door and discharge the gun in the direction of the broken window to scare bruin off for good. But he knew that would alarm the household. He found the long vigil boring but, on the whole, it seemed the proper thing to do.

The big clock downstairs struck two and three and four and five.

Nothing but the deep breathing of the four boys disturbed the silence.

Suddenly Arthur, coming out of a sleep as a swimmer pops up from a deep dive, exclaimed, "What's that? I hear something." They both listened.

"It's a car," Arthur declared.

To his intense mortification, Robin Hood heard no sound for several seconds. "But then I'm sleepy," he excused himself inwardly. And then, "That boy has an amazing sense of hearing," he added to himself.

It was a car and the sound was coming closer and closer. Staring out the window, they suddenly caught sight of the approaching automobile.

"It's Mr. Westabrook's Rolls," Robin Hood and Arthur exclaimed simultaneously.

"I'll rout that bear out now," Robin Hood exclaimed. "And I've got to be quick about it! Come on, Arthur, and watch the fun."

Fortunately the car was approaching slowly over the bumpy road.

Robin Hood rushed downstairs, Arthur after him. Robin Hood brought the gun to his shoulder, opened the door of the living room and pulled the trigger.

As "Buffalo" Westabrook and Billy Potter

slowly neared the chalet, they heard a shot.

"That came from the chalet," Mr. Westabrook said in an alarmed tone. "Who could be firing a gun indoors at this hour of the morning?"

And then to their amazement, a big black bear shot out through the window of the living room, jumped off the piazza, leaped onto the grass and, turning towards the forest back of the house, lumbered away at a high speed.

The two men watched aghast until it disappeared into the forest.

CHAPTER XVII

THE CAMP ENTERTAINS OTHER VISITORS

APPARENTLY the shot had wakened the entire household—all except Zeke and Florabelle.

Gradually the front windows upstairs filled with faces, as both the girls and boys rushed to see what had happened. Maida was the first to appear. "Oh, father! Oh, father! How glad I am to see you," she called. "But be careful, there's a bear downstairs in the living room."

"He's gone," her father reassured her. "He's on his way west. At the rate he was going, I should say he will reach Chicago by noon."

"Oh, Billy!" Maida exclaimed, "how glad I am to see you too. I wish you could have been here last night."

"I'll regret that all my life," Billy Potter exclaimed.

Billy Potter was a short, broad-shouldered young man with a thick thatch of golden hair, so curly that it defied all the efforts of barbers to straighten it. Blue-eyed and twinkled-eyed, an athlete, full of life and gaiety, he was a great favorite with the Big Eight. Maida could not remember when she had not known Billy Potter, but the Charlestown contingent of the Big Eight had known him only as long as they had known Maida. He was a reporter on a New York paper.

In no time whatever, all the inmates of the chalet were downstairs, the girls with bathrobes over their nightgowns and the boys with bathrobes over their pajamas, shaking hands with the two newcomers and telling them in a variety of versions, Rosie's and Arthur's adventure with the bear and the long siege of the night. Presently, all dressed and looking as fresh as daisies, appeared Mrs. Dore and Bunny. Scarcely had they arrived on the spot when sounds from the kitchen indicated that Zeke and Florabelle were getting breakfast.

Presently, still full of excited chatter, they all sat down to the table. But nobody failed to do justice to Florabelle's delicious hot biscuits and her equally delicious bacon and eggs.

"You've been awake all night, Robin Hood," Mr. Westabrook commented.

"Yes," Robin Hood answered. "Perhaps it was a mistake in judgment not to scare the bear off immediately. But I had a feeling that he would leave any moment. Instead he took a lodging for the night."

"You look pretty fit for a man who's had no sleep," Billy Potter commented.

"Oh, I can get along with surprisingly little sleep," Robin Hood said. "I'm going to call up the State Police now and warn them about the bear. And then I'll turn in for a little nap."

But before he could get to the telephone, the children started to show Mr. Westabrook the various collections they had made for him.

Nobody could have been more appreciative. Mr. Westabrook examined Laura's book of leaves and Maida's book of flowers with the utmost care, identifying many but failing lamentably on others. Rosie's socks, he declared, enchanted him as he liked particularly home-knit hosiery. He lingered longest over Silva's rainbows. "Whenever I'm discouraged, Silva," he said, "I'm going to take your book out and look at it, for such beauty is bound to raise my spirits."

Tyma's map, Arthur's diary, Harold's collection of "strange things" interested him profoundly, too. And when Dicky had played the little collection of notes, which he tried to make sound like falling water and which he had named *Cascade,* he demanded not one encore, but a half a dozen.

It was nearly noon before Robin Hood got to the telephone in the back hall. He talked for several minutes. When he came back into the living room, he was laughing. "They've already captured the bear," he explained. "It seems that, up until yesterday, he was a nice tame bear and wouldn't hurt a fly. He belongs to a farmer, ten miles on the other side of Opal Lake. He captured him when he was a cub, named him Blackie. Blackie's always been extremely good-natured. It seems he's very fond of pop and drinks it from the bottle. They keep him tied up of course. Yesterday morning, for the first time, he developed a temper. They noticed that he was surly. Somehow or other he managed to wrench himself free and made off into the forest. They didn't miss him until late yesterday afternoon. But whether he wanted some more pop, or was just plain hungry, he turned up at the farm a few minutes ago. They had already warned the State Police and they were on the lookout for him. Mr. Van Eltin says that he doesn't think he'll keep him any longer. He'll give him to a zoo. But he'll be there for a day or two and he asks us if we wouldn't like to come and visit him."

Hubbub followed this invitation.

"All right!" Mr. Westabrook agreed good-naturedly. "We'll all take a nap after luncheon and then we'll call on Mr. Bear."

And so, at three o'clock, the whole party, including Robin Hood who insisted on being waked up to go—and even Zeke and Florabelle—who, when consulted, declared they wanted to see the bear too—started off.

"This is a regular caravan," Billy Potter commented, "two beach wagons and an automobile."

They stopped at the first village to buy a supply of pop.

Mr. Van Eltin came forward to meet them as they turned into the drive.

"Blackie's been sleeping all the morning," he explained, after the introductions were over. "I expect you had to take a nap too. He's awake now, though, and he'll be delighted with that pop you've brought him."

He led the excited party around back of his barn. There, in a corral, Mr. Blackie Bear was pacing restlessly as far as his chain would let him go.

That chain could not permit him to get to the edge of the corral, but he could reach for a bottle that was held up to him through it.

"It's my bear," Rosie exclaimed sparkling and bright-eyed. "I insist on giving him his first bottle of pop."

"And quite rightly, Rosie," Mr. Westabrook approved. Rosie pulled the cap off the bottle with the little tool which the store had provided for that purpose, held the bottle between the bars. Blackie arose to his hind legs, seized it avidly and placing it in his mouth, poured the contents down his throat, threw the empty bottle away. So, one by one, at intervals, the others of the Big Eight presented Blackie with a bottle.

After a while they wandered about Mr. Eltin's farm enjoying other creatures, tamer but not quite so bibulous in their habits; beautiful Guernsey cows, a lamb that was the pet of the whole household, hens, chickens, ducks, a cat with a family of kittens which had been trained to leave the chickens and ducklings alone, and a huge old mastiff dog, who had been trained to leave the cat and her kittens alone.

They arrived at the chalet late in the afternoon. After dinner, they sat about the fire and talked. "I suppose, father," Maida said wistfully after a while, "that your coming now means that our vacation is over."

"Yes," Mr. Westabrook agreed, "that's exactly what it means."

"Oh!" quavered the Big Eight, "Oh! Oh!" For a moment their faces dropped. And then Rosie spoke in a tone that was almost bell-like, it was so clear with happiness, "But just think, we're going to see the Little House again."

"The Little House!" came in full round tones from the Big Eight. "The Little House!" "The Little House!"

"Oh, I can't wait to get home!" exclaimed Silva.

"Gee, how I'll like to go up into the Tree

House," Arthur exclaimed, "and look through the binoculars at Spectacles Island."

"And how I like to go fishing in the Magic Mirror," exclaimed Harold.

"And I'll see my grandmother and Delia!" Dicky exclaimed. "Oh boy!"

"We'll all see our fathers and mothers!" Laura reminded the Charlestown group. "Mr. Westabrook said that they would all be there to welcome us."

Their sudden sorrow at leaving Maida's Little Camp had turned into joy at the thought of seeing Maida's Little House. Nevertheless, when Mr. Westabrook said, "I think this household had better get to bed early tonight to make up its lost sleep," nobody demurred. "You know," he added, "Billy and I got up at four o'clock to make the camp early."

By half past nine the chalet was as silent as a tomb.

Mr. Westabrook stayed a whole week at Maida's Little Camp and that week was crammed with pleasant activity and the happiness that comes from it.

Again the Big Eight were united all day long because every one of them wanted to go wherever Mr. Westabrook was going, every one of them wanted to do whatever Mr. Westabrook was doing. Mr. Westabrook himself was excited over all their interests.

One morning, he walked with the Big Eight to the foot of Rainbow Waterfall, obviously finding it quite as beautiful as his companions expected. Immediately afterwards, they all climbed to the top of the cataract where again Mr. Westabrook displayed the expected enthusiasm. They took him to Opal Lake to see the beaver dam and to fish. While he was fishing, however, the girls stayed on the shore and talked, for there happened to be no real fishermen among them. They explored the forest daily. Rosie conducted him in state to the place by the brook where she had first seen the bear. She even climbed the big oak for him. Arthur, in his turn, pointed out the tree by the boulder which had offered him a haven of refuge. And not to be outdone by Rosie, he climbed to the top of the elm.

"I don't think I went up so fast this time," he admitted.

"I'm sure you didn't," Rosie declared.

It had not rained since Mr. Westabrook's arrival and the tissue confetti, which Rosie had scattered, still blazed a scarlet trail for them going and coming.

But with Mr. Westabrook in the party, they penetrated much deeper in the forest than they had ever gone before—explored new acreages of great trees. Once, indeed, they took a lunch and were gone the entire day—mountain-climbing. Mr. Westabrook had been a hunter in his youth—in the Adirondacks, in Maine and in the Far West. He told them plenty of stories of his hunting experiences as they went along.

After dinner, they always found time for croquet. Mr. Westabrook proved to be an adept at the game. Neither Robin nor Bunny were particularly adept but they improved gradually. Mrs. Dore, however, was the surprise of the group and Dicky's everlasting pride. Rapidly, she took on the Big Eight, one after another, then the grown-ups, one after another, and beat them all. The hour before dinner was always a lively one. They agreed that more than four pairs of players to a game made it a little unwieldly and so there was always eight playing and four looking on. The audience invariably took sides and the game went on to an accompaniment of applauding cheers and shouts, depreciatory hisses and groans.

There came toward the end of the week one rainy day. Insisting that they should not be restrained by anything so trifling as weather, the Big Eight went out for a walk both morning and afternoon. But that walk did not last long. There was a heavy, buffeting rain and a hard, tearing wind. It was difficult to keep in the path, difficult to see where they were going, difficult to examine anything when they got there. These walks were, of necessity, short ones. All the rest of the morning, therefore, the Big Eight devoted themselves to correspondence. By the time luncheon bell rang, there lay heaped on the table, where the mail was always placed, a pile of picture post cards and heavy envelopes, respectably high.

After their unsuccessful post-luncheon walk, the Big Eight seemed to be at a loose end. Nobody wanted to write any more letters. Nobody wanted to read. It was then that Bunny came into the living room with a big white box in her hands. She opened it and one by one took out a series of T. D. pipes. "How about a soap bubble party?" she asked gaily.

"A soap bubble party!" Silva repeated. "I never heard of such a thing. What do you do at a soap bubble party?"

"You blow bubbles," Bunny said. "The boy and girl who blow the biggest bubbles get prizes."

"Oh, I love soap bubble parties!" Laura exclaimed. "I gave one once. And what were the prizes? Oh, I remember—a doll for the girls. A doll!" she repeated scathingly. "What a silly present."

"I don't think it was silly," Rosie remonstrated, "I won it. It was a lovely doll. Your mother dressed it. It wore a Red Riding Hood cape and the hood was over its head when she gave it to me. I have it still at home."

"What was the boy's prize?" Tyma asked.

"What was it?" Laura repeated absently, obviously thinking.

"What *was* the boy's prize?" Harold questioned the past.

"You ought to remember," Laura said.

"I don't," Harold declared. "Something as silly as a doll, I suppose."

"I remember what it was," Rosie exclaimed. "It wasn't silly at all. It was a book. It was *Hans Brinker or the Silver Skates*. I hadn't read that book then, but I got it out of the library. Oh, how I loved it! When we got to the Little House I found it there and I read it all over again."

In the meantime, Bunny had cleared the center table and covered it with a big square of oilcloth. Mrs. Dore had brought in a bowl of water, in which rested a rapidly softening cake of soap. She placed a mammoth bath towel on the floor in front of the table. Then Bunny handed a pipe to everybody.

"Now we're going to blow bubbles in turn," she ruled. "We'll take our turns alphabetically. It's your turn first, Rosie, because Brine begins with B. Now remember, you must get the rim of the pipe bowl covered with soap. You must blow very slowly. And the rest of us must all keep very quiet because when the bubble gets big, the faintest movement will break it."

Rosie scraped the bowl through the soap, dipped her pipe into the bowl of water, lifted it out and began to blow. She blew slowly and steadily.

"Oh," Silva breathed, "isn't it beautiful. It's full of color. All kinds of colors. It looks as though color were pouring out of the bowl of the pipe."

The group watched fascinated. Suddenly there was a noiseless snap and the bubble had gone.

"It's like magic," Maida declared, "the way that great, big beautiful thing suddenly disappears. Oh, what a lovely game, Bunny."

Silva's chance came next. And she made a bigger bubble even than Rosie. Had Silva been creating one of the opals, which so fascinated her, she could not possibly have seemed more excited. A glow, soft as the softest candlelight, filled her eyes; color, pale as the palest tea rose petal, flooded her cheeks. After an interval, she stopped to take a breath, holding her iridescent creation up to the light. It maintained its beautiful shape an instant, its shifting hues—and then suddenly winked out. Tyma came next but he blew too hard and too swiftly. His bubble had hardly come into existence before it flashed and was gone.

Dicky and Arthur contended for next place, both having names which began with D. But fortunately for Dicky, and unfortunately for

Arthur, the second letter in Dicky's name was O and in Arthur's name U. So Dicky blew the fourth bubble. He was much crestfallen however when, having grown a diameter of about two inches, it suddenly snuffed out.

"Now that's what you get for being so greedy," Arthur jeered. But his bubble broke at a size even smaller than Dicky's.

"Who's greedy now?" Dicky commented heartlessly.

In strict alphabetical order came the rest.

"Oh, father," Maida wailed once, "what a misfortune that our name begins with W. We're way at the end of the list."

"Well, let's turn that into good fortune," Mr. Westabrook suggested. "We'll watch all the others and profit by their failures."

"Let's!" Maida smiled.

Robin Hood, of course, proved to be a master at the game. He produced the biggest bubble that had yet appeared. The Lathrops were adept too, but not quite as good as Robin Hood. Then Mr. Westabrook—coming before Maida because his name began with J and hers with M—beat Robin Hood's record. Maida tried to outdo her father, but although she produced a very creditable bubble it was not quite big enough. Last of all Bunny entered the contest. And she outdistanced them all.

"This is only a preliminary tryout," Bunny

declared. "Now we've all had a little practice, we'll try again."

The game went on and on. When finally, Bunny decided that they must make their last round of bubbles, the children discovered, to their great amazement, that most of the afternoon had gone. By now, they had learned the trick of taking a long breath first and then blowing slowly but steadily. It came down, in the end, to five contestants—Rosie, Laura, Mr. Westabrook, Robin Hood and Dicky, all of whom had gradually developed great skill.

One by one, Rosie eliminated them all from the contest, except Dicky. And in the end, Dicky won against her.

Bunny brought the prizes forward. They were extremely appropriate. For Rosie came a box filled with scented soap—three pieces in varying colors—feminine in look. For Dicky came a box of soap too, but not scented, and white in color—distinctly masculine in appearance.

"What a lovely afternoon," Maida exclaimed as the Big Eight put away the litter from the game and straightened up the room. "We must have a soap bubble party at the Little House sometime."

Perhaps it was Maida's allusion to the Little House which induced in the Big Eight a kind of homesickness. Undoubtedly the weather helped. For all the evening long, the rain beat against the windows and the wind shook the very panes in their casements.

Zeke had built up one of his big fires and the entire group sat about it.

Suddenly Dicky spoke. "I shall be glad to see the Little House again," he said wistfully. "Of course I'm wild about this camp. I certainly want to come here again sometime. But it will be fun to go bathing in waves again and salt water."

"And to see our rooms again," Laura said. "I do love it here, but our rooms at home are so dainty and beautiful."

"And the gym," Harold put in. "Going through the air on those traveling rings—gee!"

"And our flower garden!" Silva recalled softly. "We'll be having fall flowers before we know it."

"And the Little Seven," Maida added. "Oh, how I shall hug them."

"And the books," Arthur sighed. "I think I am going to read my pirate books all over again."

"And what fun it will be to market again and plan the meals on Zeke's and Florabelle's day out," Rosie exclaimed. "I'd forgotten how I thought I hated it. Now I know I really enjoyed it."

"When do we start home, father?" Maida asked.

"Day after tomorrow," Mr. Westabrook said.

"I'm glad," Maida commented solemnly.

"I guess we're all glad," Arthur declared soberly.

CHAPTER XVIII

MR. WESTABROOK MAKES AN ANNOUNCEMENT

NEVERTHELESS, despite their sudden homesick yearning for the Little House, the Big Eight veered, in the next day's sunshine, to a passionate regret at leaving Crescent Moon Camp. On the last afternoon, they visited Rainbow Waterfall, Opal Lake and all their favorite spots in the forest. After they returned to the chalet, Rosie climbed her last tree.

Then they set themselves to packing.

They made an early start the next morning, Mr. Westabrook, Billy Potter and Mrs. Dore taking the lead in the Rolls; Robin and Bunny and the Big Eight in one beach wagon; Zeke and Florabelle and most of the luggage in the other.

For an interval, after they started, the Big Eight were silent, just as, for an interval, they had been silent after leaving the Little House a month ago. But after a while, they came out of the abstraction, began to point things out to each other, to talk and laugh.

It was a beautiful day—not quite so warm

as that first day of travel early in August, for a touch of autumn filled the air with its winy tang. And now, here and there, they caught a glimpse of a tree prematurely gold or crimson. Goldenrod, tiny, white fall daisies and tiny, blue fall asters lined the roads; Joe-pieweed and milkweed. The rose-hips had turned scarlet.

The Big Eight recognized all along the way scenes which, on coming to New York, had attracted them instantly as they passed, noted scenes quite as beautiful which they had completely overlooked. Of the waterfalls, of which three times they caught glimpses, they asserted that they could not compare with Rainbow Waterfall, of the bodies of water, however big, however picturesque, that they could not compare with Opal Lake. No mountains seemed so high as those that surrounded the Little Camp; no view so beautiful as the one they had gazed on every one of their thirty precious days.

Again Mrs. Dore had put up a delicious luncheon and again they stopped at a wayside eating house where they could order hot cocoa and ice-cream. Sitting around a big, rustic table provided for the convenience of guests, they ate amazing numbers of sandwiches and hard-boiled eggs.

Zeke and Florabelle had sped ahead long ago. They were trying to make time, for they yearned to get home as soon as possible. Mr. Westabrook, who was of course driving his car, and Robin Hood, who was again driving the beach wagon, had gone with comparative slowness because they wanted the children to enjoy the beautiful scenery and because they wanted to be together at luncheon.

"Now that we've had luncheon together," Mr. Westabrook announced as they walked towards the cars, "I think probably I'll break loose and, like Zeke, try to make as good time as I can. I'd like to get to the Big House as early as possible. I want to look over my correspondence before dining at the Little House with you."

And so, the Big Eight were not surprised when they suddenly discovered that the Rolls had disappeared in the distance.

They came to the state line.

"Good-bye, New York!" Rosie exclaimed. "Greetings, my native Massachusetts!"

The Big Eight laughed. Giving an oral greeting and casting an oral farewell to geographical localities was Rosie's particular joke and somehow it always entertained the group.

However, very soon after they got into Massachusetts, a quiet descended on the Big Eight. Just as on the trip to Maida's Little Camp, Harold, Tyma and Dicky stretched themselves out on the seats and fell asleep. All four of the girls napped, leaning crazily against each other, swaying as the car swayed. In the front seat Bunny dozed, her head against a pillow made from her thick cape. But Arthur remained wide-awake, hungrily drinking in the scene, first on one side, then on the other.

After a while, the sleeping passengers began to wake up. Bunny first, with an, "Oh, what a nice nap I've had!"; the Big Eight with varying exclamations of surprise that they had slept so long and sorrow that they had missed anything. But in another moment, Rosie was saying, "Oh, we're getting towards home. I remember that pond with the islands in it. It was one of the first things I noticed."

"I'd say that we have about two hours to go," Harold declared. "What would you say, Robin Hood?"

"About that," Robin Hood agreed.

"Just think, in two hours and a half," Laura breathed, "I'll see my father and mother."

"Oh boy," Harold reinforced her enthusiasm.

"And I'll see my mother and father," Rosie Brine struck in. "And my little brother!"

"I'll see Granny and Delia," Dicky kept up with procession.

"And Tyma and I'll see Aunt Vashti and Aunt Save and Baby Nesta," Silva concluded the chorus.

"You almost make me wish that father hadn't come up to Camp," Maida sighed.

"It's so nice to see people when you've been separated. I'll try to feel as though I hadn't seen him for a year. Anyway, we'll all see the Little Seven again."

"How I'll hug Betsy!" Rosie exclaimed.

"And the darling little Clarks," Laura chimed in.

"And Molly and Timmie," Maida added. "How lucky we are to have two babies in the Little House!"

"Delia isn't really a baby any longer," Rosie declared. "After all, she must be nearly three."

"That's what my mother says," Dicky put in.

And now, impatience spread like wildfire through the Big Eight. "What time is it now?" everybody said every five minutes. Followed an immediate consultation of wrist watches.

"Do you mean to tell me," Rosie would exclaim, "that only five minutes has gone by?"

They groaned in misery over the occasional trucks which, in narrow roads, held them up; of the long lines of cars which, at the arrival of trains at railroad stations, slowed their progress; at city traffic everywhere which compelled them to consider too many red lights and which clogged the progress by the existence of so many one-way streets; and by those occasional road hogs who, by sticking fast in the middle of the road, prevented their passing.

But some way or other, the time did pass, although, more than once, Rosie insisted that it was standing still. They began to recognize towns, buildings—town halls of Georgian architecture or Colonial churches with tapering steeples; pretty commons with pools on them; beautiful streets lined with wine-glass elms and old houses.

They began to call the names of towns as fast as they passed the signposts. And all the time, they were getting nearer and closer to . . .

"South Satuit," Arthur called triumphantly, "we're almost there."

The Big Eight all leaned forward, staring at the familiar landscape.

And now, they had passed through the gates of the Westabrook estate, were bowling along the beautiful driveway. On and on! Presently, in the distance, the huge white marble cube of the Big House glimmered through the trees. Nearer and it disengaged itself from the forest. Here and there, great trees dotted the green velvet of the wide lawn. But it seemed surrounded by space. Gardens. Ponds. Peacocks. But after the first glance, all of the Big Eight continued to strain ahead. The Big House slipped into the background.

The trees, on either side, grew thicker, higher, closer together and now ahead the road opened onto green grass.

The beach wagon turned into the drive.

Ahead . . . why they might have just left it. For there they stood just as they grouped a month ago—the parents and the Little Seven. Della. Poppy. At sight of them, the Big Eight broke into cheers, and waved handkerchiefs and at the sight of the beach wagon, the group at the door broke into cheers and waved handkerchiefs too. At the sound, Mr. Westabrook appeared in the doorway with Billy Potter.

"Welcome home to the Little House, Big Eight," he called.

It would be impossible to describe the confusion that followed.

Every member of the Big Eight rushed first to his kin, hugged them and kissed them—even Arthur hugged his father. Then they kissed all the Little Seven. Delia called, "Hello!" and "Good-bye!" constantly. Nesta held out her arms to everybody, and as usual echoed Delia, "'lo!" and "'bye!" "I runned away," Betsy tried to tell everybody, dimpling with triumph. "But Poppy finded me."

Presently the hubbub died down and they were all eating dinner in the dining room together—three tablefuls of them—all, of course, except the Little Seven, who were, by this time, in bed.

"Twenty-four," Arthur exclaimed, counting carefully. "Gee, what a party!"

It proved to be a party indeed, a very special party. For at the close of the dinner, instead of giving the signal to rise, Mr. Westabrook whispered something to Zeke. Then, as Zeke left the room, Mr. Westabrook said, "I'm going to keep you here a little longer, my friends, for I have something to say to you."

In the meantime, Florabelle, Della and Poppy entered the room carrying trays of wine glasses. They placed a glass at every place. Then they returned, each with a pair of bottles. One after another—to the accompaniment of a vigorous popping—Zeke opened the bottles that he and Florabelle carried.

"Champagne!" Harold exclaimed. "Boy!"

The Big Eight watched with wonder as Zeke, Florabelle and Della poured a sparkling, pale yellow liquid into the glasses in front of the grown-ups. The champagne continued to foam in the glass for a long time; it sparkled to the last drop. But it was Poppy who filled the glasses of the Big Eight—with ginger ale.

Again Mr. Westabrook rose to his feet.

"I have a very important announcement to make to you and a very beautiful one," he began, "Bunny and Robin Hood are going to be married and I want you to drink their health."

An instant of complete, stupefied silence followed. Then the Big Eight leaped to their feet and cheered madly. The grown-ups applauded and laughed, laughed and applauded again. And then, as Bunny, blushing, dimpling, sparkling, and Robin Hood smiling but looking a little confused too, arose, Mr. Westabrook lifted his glass high.

Everybody else lifted his glass high and drank to the end of it.

CHAPTER XIX

MAIDA TAKES CHARGE

THE rest of that evening at the Little House was perpetual hubbub and clamor. Bunny and Robin Hood became the center of a kind of reception, for the people in the Little House sat about them in a circle, with the engaged pair in the center. The innermost ring was, of course, the Big Eight and from them, of course, poured the greatest number of questions.

There was hubbub and clamor, too, the next morning, though briefer and of a different kind. First, the parents left for Charlestown. Deeply tanned—even richly sunburned, some of them, after a month in the Little House—they were well and happy all of them. The instant, after many volleys of good-bye hugs and kisses, they had all departed, Maida, starry-eyed with excitement, asked, "Bunny, could we all talk with you for a little while and you, too, Robin Hood? There are some questions I would like to ask you."

"Certainly," agreed Bunny. "Let's come right into the living room now."

In another minute, Bunny and Robin Hood were seated on one of the big couches and the Big Eight, all but Maida looking a little puzzled, were grouped about them.

Maida began at once. "I want to ask you one question—two very important questions," she said in a voice which faltered slightly, "and then to make one very important suggestion. When the idea first came to me, it frightened me. Then I began to get my courage back. But now that I must say it, I begin to be frightened again."

"Now, Maida," Bunny remonstrated, "the idea of you being afraid of me."

"I'm not really afraid of you, Bunny," Maida declared, slipping on to the floor in front of the bride-to-be and taking one of the little hands in both of hers, "so I'll go right on. One question is—what kind of a wedding is it going to be and the other—what are you going to wear?"

"I'm so glad you asked these questions," Bunny approved warmly, "because I was just going to tell you all about it. Last night I spoke with all your parents, but in the excitement I didn't get any chance to talk with you. First off, the wedding is going to be in the Episcopalian Church in Satuit."

"The one Mr. Westabrook gave the Communion Service to," Arthur asked, "the one we found buried on Spectacles Island?"

"Yes," Bunny answered. "It is a little church, as you all know, and a very beautiful one. You see, Big Eight, in the Episcopalian marriage service, someone must always give the bride away to her bridegroom. Generally, it is a father, an uncle, or a brother, even a mother or an aunt, some near relative anyway. I have told you that I am an orphan and that I have no near relatives at all and not even any distant relatives who live in the East. And so, Mr. Westabrook is going to give me away."

"Oh, how happy that will make father," Maida exclaimed. And then as everybody laughed, "I didn't mean that it will make him happy to give you away, but he'll be delighted to be important at your wedding."

"Now, ordinarily," Bunny went on, "the wedding procession consists of—oh, there may be a lot of people—a best man, a maid of honor, bridesmaids and ushers. Robin decided that Billy Potter must be his best man and I, that my roommate at college, Barbara Barnes, must be my maid of honor. We have chosen the ushers from Robin's friends and mine. You girls of the Big Eight are to be bridesmaids and you, boys—I don't know just what to call you. I'll use an old-fashioned word, groomsmen. The two little Clarks with Betsy and Molly will be flower girls. And Timmie will be the ring bearer. He will carry the wedding ring on a cushion."

"Oh!" variously exclaimed the girls of the Big Eight. "How lovely!" "How I shall love to be a bridesmaid!" "What fun it's going to be!"

The boys said nothing. In fact they looked a little appalled. Tyma even turned pale.

"Now don't get frightened, boys," Bunny reassured them. "It is nothing to do."

"The whole thing won't last more than ten or fifteen minutes," Robin explained. "All you have to do is to walk up the aisle, two by two, and then walk back again, two by two."

"Just like the animals going into the ark!" Arthur commented, smiling feebly.

"Exactly," Robin Hood agreed.

"I'll do it," Arthur announced, "but I'd almost rather face a bear in the Adirondacks," he ended ruefully.

"But think of me, Arthur," Robin Hood put in, laughing. "I've got to do all sorts of things. I've got to remember when to say 'Yes' and when to say 'I do.' I've got to remember about that ring. If you boys don't stand by me, I don't know what kind of a boner I'll pull."

"We'll stand by you," Arthur protested.

"What are we going to wear, Bunny?" Laura asked.

"I hadn't quite decided," Bunny said a little uncertainly; "I thought that I would talk that over with you. The boys, I know, will

—not a big one, but ample enough, for their wants were simple. Rarely did they leave the Big House except to wander through the woods and to make excursions to the ocean. The girls, it was true, went once a week to Satuit Center to market. It was their job to do the cooking on Thursday, for that was a holiday for the entire household crew. That day, the Big Eight cooked and served the meals. Almost never did the Big Eight go to Boston. It was surprising how their allowances mounted up, for there was so little temptation to spend it.

It was Arthur who broke the silence. "I propose that we all put in a whole month's allowance towards the wedding present."

"That would be very nice," Maida agreed instantly. "We should be able to get something perfectly beautiful with that."

"It must be perfectly beautiful," Silva insisted. "Something very, very *precious*—but I haven't the faintest idea what."

"You tell us what, Maida Westabrook," Rosie commanded. "I know you have thought it all out. And I know you thought of the most perfect thing anyone could think of. Because that's the kind of a girl you are."

Rosie marched over to Maida's side, gave her a swift hug and returned to her chair.

"Thank you, Rosie," Maida said, looking a little startled, "but you are right. I have thought of something. And I'll tell you what made me think of it. Do you remember, one morning, when we were at Camp Crescent Moon, Bunny was a little late in getting up? We all ate our breakfast first, but Robin Hood waited for her. They had their coffee together on the piazza."

"I remember perfectly," Laura declared. "I wonder that I did not realize that they were in love then. They seemed so happy talking and laughing together."

"Last night when I was thinking this over," Maida went on, "I suddenly saw that picture of them drinking their coffee together on the piazza and I thought it would be nice if we gave them a silver coffee pot and a half dozen coffee cups."

"Oh!" Silva approved, "I think it would be wonderful."

"So do I!" approved Rosie.

"It's perfect," exclaimed Laura.

"I remember," Maida continued, "that my mother liked to drink her coffee out of a cup of very thin china. She said she liked to see the coffee through the cup. It was porcelain—not china—I remember. I thought we'd get some porcelain cups. But you boys haven't said anything," she remonstrated. "Do you like the idea?"

"I think it's swell," Arthur answered for the four boys. "Let's go up to Boston as soon as we can and pick out the coffee pot and the cups. Let's go tomorrow."

"The sooner the better," Maida declared, "because as the wedding gets closer and closer, we'll get busier and busier. I'll telephone the Big House and ask if we can go uptown in the beach wagon."

Maida telephoned at once. It happened that Mr. Westabrook had not left the house. He listened to her plans with approval and gave his permission for the expedition to Boston.

But getting the present was not as easy as it looked. Finding the cups was simple, for they went to the famous china shop, from which Mr. Westabrook had always bought his china. There, out of many specimens, they chose cups and saucers of a creamy porcelain, rimmed with gold. But when it came to the coffee pot . . . The Big Eight was united on one point. The coffee pot must be of solid silver. But nowhere could they find one that was within their means. Not even when Rosie suggested the contribution of a second month's allowance and Dicky, a third. Solid silver, they found, was extremely expensive.

"Let me talk with my father tonight," Maida said as the rather woebegone Big Eight climbed into the beach wagon to go home.

"I'm coming over to the Little House now," Mr. Westabrook announced after Maida had told him her story over the telephone. "Tell the Big Eight to hold everything. I think I have an idea."

When, after dinner, Mr. Westabrook entered the Little House, he was carrying a bundle. "Now," he explained gathering the Big Eight about him, "I'm going to drive a bargain with you. And it's going to be a hard bargain," he declared sternly, smiling about at the circle of serious faces. "You all know that in the Big House there are several collections like silver and china and glass."

The Big Eight nodded.

"Perhaps you also know," Mr. Westabrook informed them, "that one of those collections is of Paul Revere silver. When Paul Revere wasn't warning the people that the British were coming, he was a silversmith and a good one."

The Big Eight nodded again. "Robin Hood showed your collection to us, once," Arthur vouchsafed, "and told us all about Paul Revere."

"It happened once," Mr. Westabrook went on, "that at an auction, I bought a pig in a poke. That is to say, I bought a collection of things speculatively—not knowing what they all were. I was sure only of one thing—and that was a Paul Revere sugar bowl. When I got the stuff home it all proved to be worthless except for the sugar bowl and one other thing—a coffee pot in English Georgian silver. Now

I don't collect English silver and so, I have no need for that particular coffee pot. It is just about twice as valuable as the Paul Revere sugar bowl. I thought I could sell it to you to give to Bunny and Robin Hood."

He pulled the drawstring of the flannel bag he was carrying and pulled from it . . .

"Oh, father," Maida exclaimed, "it's beautiful."

All the rest of the Big Eight admired the coffee pot too. Their taste had been quickened by life among beautiful objects. Maida alone, however, could list the points which made this an especially precious specimen.

"What will it cost us, father?" Maida finally asked in a businesslike tone.

Her father laughed. He told her what he paid for the "pig in a poke." "I think it would be perfectly fair to charge you half of that. It's the biggest bargain I ever got and I'm sharing my luck with you."

The price came to a little more than the month's allowance, minus what they had paid for the cups. But they were all happy to contribute from their next month's allowance. Arthur collected the money and handed it over to Mr. Westabrook. "You'll have to trust us for the rest," Arthur said.

"All right," said Mr. Westabrook, his eyes twinkling, "thirty days' credit is customary in my business. Suppose I take this up to town tomorrow," he suggested, dropping the coffee pot back into the bag, "and see about getting Bunny's initials engraved on it."

"Couldn't we put Robin Hood's initials on it, too?" Maida asked.

"It used to be customary to use the bride's initials only," Mr. Westabrook answered. "But I think it would be very nice to have Robin Hood's there too."

"I think it will be perfect that way," Laura reinforced Maida.

And it was so ordered.

CHAPTER XX

THE LITTLE HOUSE CELEBRATES A WEDDING

THE wedding day was perfect.

"Not too hot," Rosie described it jubilantly, "not too cool. Just the one we'd have chosen."

The Big Eight thought that they had seen excitement in the Little House before, but this day they realized that they had never really known what household excitement meant. Everybody—except the Little Seven—was busy, frantically busy.

The boys of the Big Eight had spent all the afternoon before in the woods of the Westabrook estate, gathering foliage for decoration. The girls of the Big Eight spent the early morning in their garden, gathering flowers. By nine o'clock, the entire Big Eight had gone to the church and were busy decorating.

They came back to the Little House for an early lunch. Immediately afterward, they began to get ready. The wedding was to be at three. First of all, the grown-ups dressed. Then the Big Eight dressed. Then, between them, the grown-ups and the Big Eight dressed the Little Seven, for even Delia and Nesta, being good children, were going to the wedding.

All this time, Bunny remained in her room. The girls of the Big Eight had made her promise, first of all, that she would not tell them anything in detail about her wedding dress; second, that she would not show it to them when the dressmaker finished it; third, that she would not let them see her in it until she appeared in the church. And so, it happened by careful planning, that all the people, big and little, of the Little House—three carloads of them—left for the church before Bunny. Mrs. Dore remained to accompany her.

At the church, the Big Eight separated from the grown-ups, went into the Sunday School room adjoining the church. Ushers escorted Granny Flynn—and presently, Mrs. Dore—to a front pew. Around them, already seated, were Mr. and Mrs. Lathrop, Mr. and Mrs. Brine, Mr. and Mrs. Doyle, Mr. and Mrs. Clark, Mr. and Mrs. Hale, and Mr. Duncan. Zeke, Florabelle, Della and Poppy took places in the pew back of them. Back of all came pewsfull of all the people who worked at the Big House.

The rest of the pews were packed tightly with friends of the bride and groom. It was prismatic with reflections of the stained glass windows which lay like gorgeous rugs here, hung like colorful tapestry there. It was sweet with the perfume of flowers, murmurous with talk. Presently it began to vibrate to the full deep voice of the organ. The murmur died down.

The instant the music started, Bunny appeared in the Sunday School room.

"Oh, Bunny!" every one of the Big Eight exclaimed. Even the boys exclaimed. "Oh, Bunny," Maida breathed again, almost without voice, "how beautiful you look!" "You look like a princess in a fairy tale," Rosie added. "I feel that I would like to write a poem about you, Bunny," Laura took it up, "if I could only write poetry." "You look like a lovely silver bird in a cage made of a white cloud," Silva concluded.

The boys added no comments to their first exclamations. But their silence was not lack of appreciation. They were too surprised—and too moved—to speak.

Bunny's wedding dress was of a silver lace with a flower and vine pattern, so long that it streamed far back of her on the crimson velvet carpet. "Just like Bubbles Brook," Laura said. The veil, caught on her head with orange blossoms, gushed all about her and spread in great flowing billows over the train. "Just like Rainbow Waterfall," Silva said. Train and veil succeeded in making Bunny seem much taller than she was. She carried a bouquet of white violets, tied with narrow white velvet ribbons.

"Somehow, Bunny," Dicky said, finding his voice, "you look different. I don't know how."

"It's because I'm so happy, Dicky darling," Bunny explained softly. And suddenly her sparkling blue eyes grew more sparkling with the tears that filled them. She controlled herself, however, smiled until the tears dried.

Mr. Westabrook appeared, wearing clothes that nobody but Maida had ever seen him wear before—a frock coat, trousers with a faint stripe, a grey ascot tie with a pearl stickpin, grey gloves, grey spats, a tall glossy hat, a gardenia in his buttonhole. He looked very handsome and distinguished.

"What a beautiful bride!" Mr. Westabrook exclaimed. "I feel as if I were giving away the queen of the fairies. Are you all set, Big Eight?"

"All set," the Big Eight agreed.

"All set, bride?" Mr. Westabrook inquired further.

"All set," the bride answered.

"Then, what about you getting married, Bunny," Mr. Westabrook suggested smiling.

He offered Bunny his arm. Outside, in the church, the air filled suddenly with the gay, glorious strains of *Here Comes the Bride*. The procession formed swiftly and in perfect order, for they had rehearsed twice in the church. They moved through the door, across the back aisle and up the central one.

First, two by two, came the eight ushers. Next came the boys of the Big Eight, dressed in their best suits—white flannel trousers, blue coats, boutonnières—a white aster against a maple leaf. Back of the boys came the girls of the Big Eight. They wore the costumes that Maida had suggested to Bunny.

"It's going to be an autumn wedding," Maida had said. "I think it will be beautiful to have autumn coloring in our dresses."

And so, the girls wore gowns, made layer upon layer, of a fabric with a floating softness and thinness. Each layer was a different color, but all the tints of maple leaves—lemon yellow, burnt orange, high scarlet, deep crimson; all edges serrated, again like maple leaves. They wore little oval caps of velvet maple leaves in the same hues.

It must be said that never in their lives had the girls of the Big Eight looked lovelier. Maida and Laura—blonde maple leaves, their hair gleaming in gilt profusion from under their colorful caps—walked together. And Rosie and Silva—brunette maple leaves, their dark coloring made more intense by their autumn-colored gowns—walked together.

Next, trotted Timmie in a new suit of black velvet carrying very carefully a white velvet cushion on which lay the wedding ring.

Then came Bunny's maid of honor, Barbara Barnes—a tall, dark girl, very handsome and very vivacious—in yellow, a spray of white and yellow chrysanthemums in her arms.

Then, came the girls of the Little Seven, Mabel and Dorothy, walking together, Molly and Betsy. They too wore dresses of a floating thin material with serrated edges—but white. On their heads were crowns of little starlike white asters and they carried little green baskets lined with maple leaves and filled with white asters.

Last of all, appeared Bunny and Mr. Westabrook.

As they walked up the central aisle of the church, the Big Eight might well have prided themselves on the decorations. On both sides of the altar, filed autumn-tinted maple boughs—producing a screen so vivid that even the sunshot, stained glass could not dull them, yet so fragile and frail, that the leaves moved continuously in the breeze from the windows. On the altar, great silver vases held tall white asters. White satin ribbons tied great bunches of asters and autumn leaves to pew-ends. At the back of the church, maple boughs grouped in the corners.

As the procession approached the altar, the Big Eight saw that awaiting them was not only the Rev. Arthur Scrooby, tall, silver-haired, very dignified, in his white gown, but also, looking very pale and solemn, Robin Hood and beside him, looking very happy and smiling, Billy Potter.

At the altar, the procession divided into two groups. Half the ushers and the girls of the Big Eight moved to one side; the rest of the ushers and the boys to the other. Two of the little flower girls followed the girls of the Big Eight; two the boys. The maid of honor stood close to the bride; Billy Potter close to the groom; Timmie between Barbara and Billy.

Nobody noted particularly that Betsy stood just back of Timmie. But in a few minutes that fact was to become extremely important.

The music stopped. The clergyman began, "Dearly beloved," and the majestic service moved on its stately and sonorous way.

The girls of the Big Eight—and the boys too—watched avidly. They were perfectly drilled in their own minor part in the ceremony, for, in addition to the rehearsals in the church, they had held rehearsals of their own in the Little House.

"Oh," Maida had wailed again and again, "I'm so afraid that when Mr. Scrooby says, 'Who giveth this woman to be married?' my father will forget to say, 'I do.' And then if he remembers that, I'm frightened to death for fear that he'll forget, the moment he says it, to step back and sit down in the front pew."

"Oh, I don't worry one atom about your father, Maida," Rosie declared, "but I'm scared to death about Bunny. Suppose when Robin Hood starts to take her hand, she forgets to change her bouquet from her *right* to her *left* hand." Here Rosie made illustrative motions with an imaginary bouquet. "And suppose she should offer Robin Hood her left hand. Well, if that happens, I shall simply die."

"Oh, Bunny never'll forget," Arthur declared with certainty.

"Indeed. And what makes you so sure, Mr. Arthur Duncan?" Rosie demanded pithily. "Have you ever been a bride in your life?"

Arthur grinned and subsided.

"What worries *me,*" Silva admitted, "is that I'm afraid Bunny'll forget to hand her bouquet to Miss Barnes, before she and Robin Hood plight their troth."

"Well I'm nearly going crazy for fear Timmie'll drop the wedding ring," Laura sighed. "I'm going to make sure myself that there's a great dent in that cushion."

"Don't worry over that," Tyma reassured her. "I asked Billy all about it. He says that the best man always carries an extra wedding ring in his pocket for fear of just such an accident."

"Well, that's not all," Maida wailed again. "I'm so afraid, after it's all over, that Barbara will forget to arrange Bunny's veil and pull her train out straight. I wish I had all those things to do. I wouldn't forget one of them."

But none of these accidents happened, although one nearly did. All went well until the moment approached, when Robin Hood would take the ring from the cushion which Timmie bore. And then the Big Eight saw—many of the churchful of guests saw—that catastrophe was upon them. So interested had Timmie become in what was going on, that unconsciously he was allowing the white velvet cushion to tip down . . . down . . . down . . .

The Big Eight held its breath.

But these were not the only ones who saw that disaster was imminent. Betsy saw it too. With the greatest speed and resolution, she leaned forward, slipped her little forefinger through the ring and, with its tip, pinned it firmly onto the cushion. Almost immediately Robin Hood turned—and smiling in amused recognition at her presence of mind—took the ring and placed it on Bunny's finger.

A faint wave of sound ran through the church. It was not laughter, but it held amusement, also relief after strain.

The Big Eight breathed again.

Presently came from the organ, the crash of Mendelssohn's *Wedding March*. And now the procession started back. This time, however, the married pair, Bunny with her veil thrown back from her face; her hand on her husband's arm, came first. Followed Barbara Barnes with Billy Potter, both smiling; Timmie, the flower girls, the ushers, the girls of the Big Eight, the boys of the Big Eight, still very serious.

Bunny, all smiles and blushes, nodded to her friends as she walked down the aisle. And so, no longer pale but quite himself, did Robin Hood. In the Sunday School room everybody kissed the bride. Mr. Westabrook kissed her. The children of the Little House kissed her—and with due regard for her veil—hugged her. All the girls kissed and hugged Robin Hood, too, but the boys contented themselves with shaking his hand vigorously. Presently they were all in automobiles, racing to the wedding reception at the Little House.

What an afternoon it was! Guests kept arriving until both sides of the roads all around the house were parked with motors half-way to the Big House. Inside the Little House, flowers grouped everywhere—flaming autumn blooms that filled it with color. Outside on the lawn, a caterer had erected a marquee, had covered the long tables in it with delicious things to eat and drink.

Bunny insisted on keeping the Big Eight near her, so that they could meet all her friends. But after everybody had met and everybody was beginning to flock about the marquee, the Big Eight found a quiet corner to sit together. There they ate something of everything—and a good deal taken in mass—that the long table of goodies offered. The bride and groom did not seem to eat anything. The tail of her gown and her wedding veil over her arm, Bunny went with Robin Hood from group to group until she had talked with everybody. Then suddenly she disappeared. "The bride's gone to get dressed!" somebody exclaimed. "Barbara's gone too. Don't let them get away without our knowing it."

All the young girls crowded into the tiny hall of the Little House, filled the doorways of the Map Room and the Book Room, crowded the steps of the little vestibule, lined the stepping-stones which led across the lawn from the entrance to the drive.

The Big Eight began at once to pass packages of confetti among the guests.

Presently an automobile, Zeke at the wheel, appeared at the end of the stepping-stones. Immediately Bunny, with Robin Hood behind her, came flying down the stairway. She threw her bouquet over the bannister. Barbara caught it—proving, according to superstition, that she would be married before the year was out.

Bunny, in a suit of dark blue with a little rose-trimmed hat, dark blue too, with a veil, rushed through two lines of wedding guests, who volleyed confetti over her. Robin Hood dashed beside her. As he caught sight of them, Zeke opened the door to the car. The honey-mooners leaped into the automobile, the Big Eight pelting after them as fast as they could run, flooding the fugitives with confetti. But Zeke was quicker than they. The motor, which he had kept running, started up. It whirled off . . .

"They're gone!" Maida exclaimed.

CHAPTER XXI

THE FUTURE GLOWS BRIGHT

THE bride and bridegroom were already several hours away on their honeymoon. All the guests, except the parents of the Big Eight, had gone. They had stayed on at Mr. Westabrook's express invitation.

The big household had eaten their late dinner—very simple after the long work of the long day. And now the parents were awaiting the motors which would take them back to Charlestown. They sat, leaning back, comfortably relaxed, in the big chairs in the living room. Mr. Westabrook in the centre of the group, the Big Eight on the floor at their parents' feet.

Outside it had become suddenly cold. Zeke had built a fire and now the leaping flames seemed to be fighting each other in the big fireplace. Della and Poppy removed the coffee cups and all the grown-ups settled back comfortably in their big chairs, awaiting the talk that they knew Mr. Westabrook was going to give them.

He began at once.

"I've asked you all to stay," Mr. Westabrook came straight to his point, "because I have something to say to every one of you parents. Of course, you guess that it's about your children. That is true. It *is* about your children. And I want them to hear it too. It is quite as important to them as it is to you—perhaps more so."

He paused and glanced about the half-circle of listening faces. There was a look of intense absorption on every one of them. He went on.

"I hope you remember that before the Big Eight went to Camp Crescent Moon, I talked with you all about the future. I told you that Bunny and Robin Hood and Billy Potter and myself were all studying your children with the idea of finding out what we could make of them, or rather what they could make of themselves. Well, we've come to some conclusions since then. And I want to tell them to you. I want to know what you think of them of course. But I also want to know what the Big Eight think."

Mr. Westabrook paused again and again looked about the semi-circle. The children's eyes held so intently on his—a look of definite alarm in them—that he paused to smile reassuringly before he went on.

"Ladies first! So, let me begin with Rosie. We all think that Rosie has a great executive ability which has not, as yet, found an outlet.

Unless she develops a special ambition, we propose sending her to college. She may find out, before she gets to college age, that she would prefer a particular training—business, household economics, nursing. Whatever it is, however, she shall follow her own bent. How does that strike you, Mrs. Brine? And how does it strike you, Rosie?"

"I agree with every word you say, Mr. Westabrook," Mrs. Brine declared. "And I know Rosie will."

"Yes, I do, sir," Rosie declared. "I do. I don't know yet just what I want to be and I do want to think it over for a long, long time. Thank you, Mr. Westabrook."

"Now, Laura," Mr. Westabrook went on, pausing to smile affectionately at Rosie. "It is pretty evident to all of us that Laura loves dancing more than anything else. Isn't that true, Laura?"

"It certainly is, Mr. Westabrook," Laura answered. "I would like to be a great dancer."

"Well, then," Mr. Westabrook went on, "when the time comes, I think Laura should have the best instruction in dancing in the country. Do you agree with that, Mrs. Lathrop?"

"Yes, decidedly!" Mrs. Lathrop said. "But I think she should keep on with her dancing training now."

"She will have that," Mr. Westabrook promised, "all the time—the best individual training that we can get for her."

"Oh, I'm so happy!" Laura breathed.

"And we're so happy, Mr. Westabrook," Mrs. Lathrop echoed.

"And while we're on the subject of Lathrops, let's take up Harold," Mr. Westabrook suggested. "Harold has puzzled me for a long time. Not because he did not have ability, but because he has so much. General, all-round ability. Executive ability. We observed, too, that Harold was a natural commander and leader. We noted that he liked outdoor life, and that he took naturally to discipline. Then suddenly, one day, Robin Hood said 'West Point' and I felt at once that that was right. And so, if that meets with the approval of all three of you, all four of you, for I include Laura, and if he can pass his examinations, I'll try to get Harold into West Point."

"It's perfect," Mrs. Lathrop gasped. "Oh, I never thought—"

"Nothing could be better for the boy," Mr. Lathrop declared with a gratified accent.

"Oh, wouldn't that be great," Laura exclaimed, "having a brother at West Point!"

"And what about you, Harold?" Mr. Westabrook asked.

Harold had turned pale. "I like it so much that I can't speak," he gasped.

"That's all right," Mr. Westabrook reassured him. "Don't speak. Silva comes next, Aunt Save and Aunt Vashti," Mr. Westabrook took up his story. He bent sideways so he could smile at the two gypsy aunts.

The gypsy aunts smiled back at him. The firelight winked in Aunt Vashti's necklace of golden coins and in Aunt Save's silver jewelry, but neither gold nor silver was brighter than their glowing, brown gypsy eyes.

"We all have guessed that Silva likes to paint more than anything else," Mr. Westabrook asserted. "Isn't that true, Silva?"

"Oh, Mr. Westabrook," Silva exclaimed, "you know it is."

"Yes," Mr. Westabrook admitted, "I don't guess it—I know it. So, with the permission of you two, Aunt Vashti and Aunt Save, we'll begin serious instruction in art with Silva. We think she has real talent. And if the experts think so too, there is no reason why she should not finish off her training in Paris."

"Paris!" Silva breathed, clutching Maida's hand, as though to hold herself from floating away.

"Paris!" Maida breathed, clutching Silva's arm, as though to hold her from flying off.

"Now before you speak, Aunt Vashti and Aunt Save," Mr. Westabrook went on, "let's talk about Tyma. Tyma loves the sea. He wants to live on the sea. And so, I'm thinking of sending him to one of those schools where they train boys to be officers in the merchant marine. But he'd have to work extremely hard to meet their standard. How would you like that, Tyma?"

"Like it!" Tyma gasped. "Like it?" He stuttered, spluttered, gulped and choked.

Everybody laughed.

"You don't have to say anything more, Tyma," Mr. Westabrook gentled him. "And so, if it's all right with your aunts, we'll proceed along those lines."

"It sure is all right with me," quavered old Aunt Vashti. "As long as he doesn't ask me to go with him. Gypsies belong on land."

"And it is certainly all right with me," declared plump Aunt Save. "Just so long," she added, "as he gets to be President of the United States."

Everybody laughed, Tyma hardest of all.

"Well, then," Mr. Westabrook began again, "that leaves only one girl—my own troublesome daughter, Maida. And I admit to you, I haven't the remotest idea what to do with her." He smiled affectionately in Maida's direction.

"But I do," Maida said quietly, a strong note of determination in her voice. "I know exactly what I want to do. I want to go both to a regular college and to business college."

"*Business college!*" Mr. Westabrook repeated, aghast.

"Yes," Maida affirmed, "and for the best

reasons in the world. You have told me, many, many times, father, that when I am twenty-one, I shall come into the money my mother left me and that I must learn to manage my own affairs. I want to learn how to do that. I want to learn awfully. But I want to learn scientifically. First, I'd like to go to college where they'd teach me about banks and banking and stocks and bonds and rents and interest and—oh, dozens of things I've hear you talk about. Then, I'd like to go to a business college. I want to learn stenography and typewriting."

It was Mr. Westabrook's turn to stutter and splutter, to gulp and gasp. At the same time, he was thinking hard and swiftly.

Mr. Westabrook adored his daughter, but that love did not prevent him from looking at her critically, of judging her dispassionately just as he judged the other children. Arthur, he knew, was abler than Maida, Rosie more capable, Silva and Dicky more talented. He had often wondered how much the long invalidism of her childhood had set back her development, had handicapped her otherwise. But in the weeks preceding the wedding, something had happened that filled him with pride and joy. Always before, lingering in the background, listening to the others, following their leadership, Maida suddenly snapped into leadership. To her father's amazement, Maida had engineered many difficult social situations—but all with her customary simplicity and modesty. Suddenly, it seemed to him that she had become her mother.

"I never was so surprised in my life, Maida," Mr. Westabrook declared, finally. "But I think it's a good idea, and I'm for it."

"And when I come out of my business course," Maida went on steadily, "I want you to give me a job in your office."

"Better and better!" Mr. Westabrook approved. "And will I be a stern boss!"

Everybody laughed again.

"Next we come to Dicky," Mr. Westabrook went on with his story. "Of course, you all know what it is with Dicky. I don't have to tell any of you that. It's music. You're sure of that yourself, Dicky, aren't you?"

"Sure," Dicky repeated. His emphasis was solemn, but his face was luminous with joy.

"In a few days I'm going to take Dicky to the best piano teacher in Boston," Mr. Westabrook declared. "He's a big man and I shall be guided by his advice. I don't have to ask Granny Flynn or Mrs. Dore about that plan because we've talked it over many times. What I want to know is, do you like it, Dicky?"

"Do I?" Dicky repeated. "Do I? Oh boy!"

"Last, but far from least, Arthur," Mr. Westabrook declared, smiling. "You've been very patient, Arthur, waiting all this time without a word. But I think your patience is going to be rewarded. Mr. Duncan, I'm going to send Robin Hood off on some expeditions into the Southwest and Yucatan. Now I don't want to interfere with Arthur's education. We are agreed that he ought to go to college. But during the long summer vacation—with your permission—I'm going to send him to join Robin Hood and Bunny wherever they are."

"Fine!" Mr. Duncan ejaculated. "Fine! Fine! And what do you say, my lad?" He turned to his son. "Speak up, boy!"

But Arthur could not speak up. He sat paralyzed—a very statue of wonder and joy. The understanding Mr. Westabrook saw exactly what was happening. "Don't say anything now, Arthur," he commanded, "we'll talk later."

But Arthur came out of his paralysis. He leaped to his feet, rushed over to Mr. Westabrook and shook his hand. Then, dropping on the couch beside Mr. Duncan, he buried his face in his father's shoulder. Big convulsions of emotion shook his body, but he made no sound.

Excitement! Everybody talking. Everybody talking all at once. All trying to talk to Mr. Westabrook. And all trying to talk to each other.

"The best of it is," the Big Eight said in one way or another and many times over, "that we don't have to leave the Little House for a long time yet."

Presently the motors arrived—the Lathrops' own car and the big Rolls which was to take the Brines and Mr. Duncan back to Charlestown and to drop Aunt Vashti and Aunt Save at the gypsy camp. Everybody hugged everybody else in a very fury of happy farewell.

Mr. Westabrook stayed on, after the last grown-up guest had departed; for he knew the Big Eight were a little too excited to go to bed at once. He himself said little, but he listened as, one after the other, they tried to tell him how thrilled they were and how grateful. Presently he saw that the long day, the long work and the long excitement was beginning to wear on them. Finally he arose and shaking hands all around he left for the Big House.

For a moment, the Big Eight stood, gazing into the fire, saying nothing—their faces bright with happy thought.

Granny Flynn had long ago gone to bed. But Mrs. Dore, of course, was still up.

"Well, children," she said cheerily, "I think we'll have to call this a day."

"And such a day!" Arthur declared as he put the screen before the fire.

"Good night, all," everybody said.

"Good night, all," everybody answered.

The girls started upstairs to their bedrooms above. The boys started towards the New Wing.

Arthur stopped suddenly in his tracks. "Oh, Maida, what happy lives you've—" he began.

Arthur wanted to say, "What happy lives you've given us all!" But shyness prevented him from ending his sentence.

"Oh, Arthur," Maida echoed, smiling, "What a happy life you've—"

Maida wanted to say, "What a happy life you've all given me!" But she could not finish her sentence either.

Another chorus of "good nights" filled the air, as the Big Eight disappeared.

The fire was almost dead. But for a few minutes, the thin, charred logs, almost burned-out now, flickered and whispered. Then they broke and fell in a shower of sparks, dulled finally to grey ash.

Quiet fell on the Little House.

See Next Page →

You'll love Maida's next thrilling adventure, MAIDA'S LITTLE VILLAGE. Don't miss this exciting story of how the Big Eight restore the beauty of a deserted village and solve the mystery threatening their kind neighbors.

Maida's Little Shop
Primrose Court
Massachusetts
House Rock
Fairy Ring
Tree House
The Little House
Road to Maida's Little Camp in the Adirondacks
The Big House
The Stonecrop
Tilestone Hollow
Boy's House
Mess Hall
Girl's House
Tilestone Lane
Old Mill
MILL ROAD
Post Office
Brick House
The Barn